FLOWER OF MEMORY

AN AMARANTH PREQUEL

DAVID M. SNOW

FLAME ARROW PUBLISHING

SYNOPSIS

*An underwater ark that shelters the last remaining
survivors.
A young doctor tormented by his past.
A mysterious power that could drive them into
madness.*

A cataclysmic Flood has forced the survivors to retreat into an intergenerational ark, secluded from the world they have always known. But the wait is insufferable in the abyss of the Great Ocean. More than a century, heavy with silence, has passed.

The Surface is but a timeworn dream. A forgotten memory.

But Skyler Goldberg is not ready to give up. Even if it means losing everything.

Can a single man show the Archeans the path to redemption in a world abandoned by its creator?

Flower of Memory is the prequel of the dystopian science-fiction series Amaranth. Fans of the TV series The 100 and Snowpiercer will enjoy every page!

Flower of Memory (Amaranth #0.5)

Printed in Canada

First Printing: 2022

Legal Deposit: 2022

Published by Flame Arrow Publishing

ISBN 978-1-990368-12-7

www.flamearrowpublishing.com

www.davidmsnow.com

*To my significant other, who reminds me to
Treasure every moment, and to
Create memories worth living for.*

1

It's snowing in the Gardens of Humankind tonight.

Crystal shards frozen in delicate arabesque patterns are blown around by the faulty ventilation system. At another time, snow really existed.

What did their ancestors who actually set foot on solid ground think when they saw these snowflakes hail down onto their fields, their roads, the roofs of their houses, and their faces as they made their way to work? A bother to most, but a wonder to those who gaped at the winter landscape and captured it through brushstrokes and snapshots that now tell the story of the past.

Like these flowers.

Kneeling, Skyler gingerly brushes away some snowflakes settled on the red petals of a survivor among her dying sisters, who spread their bushy globes of pollen now wandering the outer reaches of the park in search of a new patch of unconquered land. All of this sounds familiar, doesn't it?

But there is far more than meets the eye to these flowers. They are the reflections of the Ark's passengers: beautiful, yet intricate, their intentions camouflaged in wafts of intoxicating scents. Their resilience is truly admirable despite the harsh weather! Under the right conditions, they spread where the wind carries them, but without proper care, they are forsaken, their beauty but a fleeting memory.

Skyler gets up. The passengers of this vessel count on him to provide comfort, heal, and save them from death's clutches. At the bottom of the Great Ocean, death can strike at any moment to silence them into mere memories, doomed to fade into oblivion. Just like the fog of his breath vanishing into thin air.

That is the weight of his responsibility, since he will be able to work at Med Bay after tomorrow's graduation which will make it all official. His classmates are celebrating tonight, but he is not in the mood. Instead, he's preparing for his new role as a commander waging battle against invisible microorganisms: sometimes he will win, others he will have no choice but to surrender. This is what doctors do behind the white curtain.

He startles at the shouts.

Skyler lies in wait, concealed perfectly in the artificial woodland. It could be some classmates from the Academy drinking ahead of tomorrow's ceremony. All it takes is a well-positioned family with the right connections to get their hands on some alcohol from the Ark's restaurant. Better yet, it could be one of the famous liquors that divers sometimes retrieve from the underwater cities' rubble. They are so rare that reports of their discovery spread very quickly. But, ever since a diver was poisoned with the contents of a three-hundred-year-old bottle, the Delta Department and Med Bay have been analyzing their contents to make sure they are harmless. The process can be slow, like everything else that has to do with the Deltas. Meanwhile, the rumor mill goes into overdrive. Who could keep secrets older than the Ark to themselves?

No doubt. There must be students drinking up their excitement at finally being able to become driving forces on this vessel and take part in the joint effort to survive. Skyler is almost envious, but tonight he just isn't feeling the thrill he should. Too much hangs in the balance for him to mindlessly indulge in unbridled fantasies. The problems will not disappear overnight, swallowed by the intoxicating effects of alcohol.

Skyler wanders off to the thicker canopy of the wooded area, now home to the first blanket of snow born of the ventilation system's failure. The hard-to-preserve vegetation will suffer, but the century-old trees give him the comfort he needs to face the future that awaits him after the graduation ceremony. Expectations are rather high for him.

Like Tamara Goldberg, the daughter of Augustus and Silvia, who were the first generation of Goldbergs to board the Ark, he wants to become a trusted surgeon in Med Bay. As the Flood shook the world, she patched together an army of Paragon guards who sacrificed themselves so that as many survivors as possible could find refuge on the Ark. To this day, Tamara Goldberg's expertise is taught at the Academy to medical students like Skyler, and his ancestor's notoriety is a difficult torch to bear.

One would think that being a descendant of Tamara would earn him favor—or at least respect—from his teachers, but it didn't. He was forced to work harder than the others, but he never complained. At least, during the time he spent studying how to repair a faulty heart valve or unraveling the possible applications of gene therapy, he wasn't stuck in the family cabin, the very antithesis of freedom in such a vast ocean.

At the bough of the massive oak tree used as a landmark in this oversized wooded area, a sudden commotion disrupts the almost wintry calm that had settled in. Paragon uniforms. Are they here to catch the revelers? Perhaps they had the nerve to snatch a legendary bottle of liquor, after all. Otherwise, the Paragon would leave them alone at this hour, especially in these parts, which are not the most popular among the passengers—

much to Skyler's relief, who comes here to escape from the mind-numbing reality. But not tonight.

Skyler puts as much distance as possible between himself and the unforgiving Paragon. Since the Ark's inception, the Paragon has had plenty of opportunities to flaunt its power in the name of justice. The last thing Skyler wants is to antagonize those who will rebuild on the Surface when the time comes.

Someone with a dazed look staggers out of the brush in a flurry of leaves and twigs.

"Emily! What on earth are you doing here?" shouts Skyler, stunned. She wipes the sweat off her forehead, and she gives him a worried look.

"I'll explain later. Just run!"

Shouts are coming their way. Too late to back out now. No matter what his best friend did, the Paragon agents will give them a hard time. The only time a family's reputation is worthless is during an interrogation.

The Gardens of Humankind become a winding, slippery maze topped with a thin layer of snow. Their breathing matches as they run, and Skyler curses at his unsteady footing that may send him stumbling at any moment. He doesn't have Emily's flexibility, who secretly trained with her father her entire childhood. Except for their occasional visits to the diver-hunters' pool, no one bothers with giving teenagers a proper training regimen. It's a privilege reserved for Paragon recruits.

Emily gets a head start on Skyler, despite slowing down so he can catch up. The agents are still concealed in the woods, and Skyler keeps running, not knowing if they are drawing near. He ducks under a dangling branch at the last moment and deftly slips toward his best friend until he can go back to running.

"Not bad for a doctor who has his nose stuck in a book all day!"

"Tell me about it. We won't outrun them so easily."

"I've got an idea."

Emily yanks his arm with startling strength as shots echo off a tree trunk, and they dash at full speed.

What the hell did she do to draw the Paragon into a fight? Emily may be reckless, but she's not stupid.

They pop out near an air vent blasting a howling blizzard. Their startled shouts blend into the din of the ventilation blades. Visibility is almost nil in this snowed-in area of the park, and Skyler feels like he's swimming in frigid water. Why is nobody turning off those vents? The park is supposed to preserve the Earth's native flora, not bury them under heaps of snow! Something's not right.

"Where's the west exit again?" asks Emily, placing a hand on his shoulder once they've retreated behind an oak tree that blocks the brunt of the storm.

Skyler crouches down to clear the blanket of snow smothering a bed of chrysanthemums. The exit shouldn't be far.

"This way," he replies, as he recalls the many times he's been in this area, wondering if one day he should grow his own garden.

Chrysanthemums would have been perfect but after all this snow, will they survive?

Near the doorway, an emergency button glows with a red halo that cuts through the snow fog. Emily has a mischievous glance, but Skyler pushes the button first.

They rush into the decontamination airlock with the blaring emergency alarm that seals off the gardens automatically: if the agents don't reach an exit in the next thirty seconds, they'll spend the night smoldering with anger.

In the warm passageway, Emily giggles under the adrenaline and squeals in victory.

"The Ark's never been so exciting," she says, her hands resting on her hips. "And I didn't think you were capable of such disregard for danger, Skyler Goldberg."

"There has to be a first time for everything," he grumbles,

dusting off the snow from his dripping hair. "Damn it! What on earth did you do to turn those Paragon agents into trigger-happy soldiers?"

"I told you, the Ark's never been so exciting. You won't believe it!"

2

The lights at the Academy are not completely out. Some areas are still bustling, such as the daycare center that watches over the children whose parents are tirelessly repairing the Ark. The need for constant maintenance shows how its framework is wearing out against the pressure of billions of liters of water. Yet the Academy does not have to deal with outdated plumbing, sloping corridors or rusted walls. Its architects took great care in building the safest and most enduring place to educate the generations that would come after the Flood. They knew what awaited the survivors and how to offer the best possible environment to learn, since no one could reach the Surface in a long while. Who knows what will be left of it once the waters recede?

The Academy is probably the cleanest part of the entire ship, and its facilities are the best kept by the Deltas. Take, for example, these holograms displaying messages to keep students abreast of their latest exams and when they will receive their final grades. Some notices even praise those whose graduation ceremony tomorrow marks the end of their studies.

Specially designed holographic displays adorn the walls, and a stream of photos with graduates wearing their family-colored uniforms floods the entrance. Skyler's is in one of the middle circles, along with the Harris's, Whites's, Yangs's, and Kay's. All these families, among others, have greatly influenced the Ark's history, and the Archeans rely on them to make their lives less painful.

"Sneaking off to the Academy right before graduation?" asks Skyler, disappointed he got dragged into Emily's wild story.

"Of course not. Well, yes, but temporarily. The Paragon won't chase us here."

There is this kind of neutrality the Sigmas advocate on the Academy's grounds. They do not tolerate any confrontation within its walls where knowledge has a sacred need for peace— a practice that has been going on since the beginning of the Ark.

"Have you been raving about the Smiths' mockery again?"

"No."

"The Yangs then? Emily, you know it's not worth it. The last time you fought back at them, your father had to get involved. They're losing their minds over their growing influence, and they'll do anything to hold their sweet spot. They know the Bateses are an easy target."

"That's the point! I've had enough of them making fun of my art projects because their so-called scientific inventions are more important."

"You've been fighting, again. How will you ever find a mentor after that? I can see it from here: Bloodthirsty artist seeks demonic master. No negative comments on my artwork allowed or a one-way trip to Dante's inferno awaits you."

"Sounds good to me," she giggles. "A swift cleansing to finish off what the Flood started."

At this point, the mentors have not yet chosen whom they will take under their wing in their respective departments for the next few years. Med Bay is an option for Skyler, the very place where he has been training so far; so is the infirmary in the command center, but until he knows which doctor will decide to mentor him, he can only speculate. If none of them choose him, he'll have to deal with administrative duties and wait for his turn next year. Reputation and grades alone are not enough to be successful on the Ark. Currying favor with people is a necessary evil. Skyler has the family background to give him a leg up, but his lack of interest in the mundane could get in the way.

While Chris Kay was courting the birthing department, Skyler was spending his time with the elderly, especially Mrs. Farrell, who bonded with him instantly and never let him out of her sight. She taught him a lot about the elderly who regularly visit Med Bay "excessively, for lack of anything better to do," as she puts it. Some of them think Skyler doesn't do enough socializing. Whatever happens, he will have to accept their decision. Worst-case scenario, he can spend quality time with Mrs. Farrell in the sanctuary, or he can sanitize the surgeon's instruments and set up syringes and vials of medicine on his cart.

Skyler balks at the idea. How did Tamara Goldberg manage to weasel her way up? Did she play along, too?

They think Skyler doesn't have the skills because he refuses to waste his time prattling on about so-called feats of modern medicine … do they even know that they are claiming other people's achievements? A quick visit to the Archives would be enough to expose them. But people don't try to sort out facts from fiction. They would much rather swallow everything they're told because it suits them, and it sounds good.

Skyler thinks back to his brand-new lab coat still sitting in its packaging. Will he ever be able to wear it and handle real cases that require the expertise he's been ingesting for the past few years? He will wear a lab coat anyway, whether it's blue or gray, but only the green color of challenge could ever satisfy him. It would show what he's really capable of—the color of the Goldbergs.

"I'm already wasting my time, anyway," adds Emily, looking at the photos distractedly. "The mentorship. But you know, I still want to honor my family despite all the crap that's been thrown at us for years."

"I know."

"Thanks for still having faith in me."

"So?"

She takes a deep breath as she watches her own photo glow on the panoramic board, in a dusty corner, far away from the middle circle that flashes red, an unbreakable barrier.

"I stayed longer to finish my final art project today. Before I left, I overheard a conversation with Instructor Paradis. She was talking about Adeline White. You know who she is, don't you?"

"No offense, but you're no match for that woman. My father told me she oversees her own labs because she refuses to work with scientists who fall under the Deltas. If you don't bear her mark, she won't even talk to you."

"Even if she offered to mentor me, I wouldn't accept. I like the power she represents, but not what she does. She obviously has no talent."

"In this world, you can't choose who you do business with, especially when it comes to your mentorship." Skyler realizes how absurd and unfair this is. As if the mentors' flair was an objective way to seal their future! If the Archeans could let go of their obsession with control, they would realize that passion is far more powerful than any inborn talent.

"Wait for it," Emily says, tapping her foot. "Adeline White holds these special soirees on occasion. No one knows about them except for her very own circle of lucky guests who can invite someone in return. Her soirees are a buzz."

"Let me guess. You want to go?" She blushes and then fails miserably to repress her smile. "I could ask my dad to find a way to get you in, but I really think it's a bad idea."

"That won't be necessary. I've already been."

"What?" says Skyler, who freezes.

"I wouldn't be wearing these clothes otherwise. My mother's dress. I knew you wouldn't notice."

"You are playing with fire. This woman has the power to destroy your reputation."

"For what's left of it, I don't care."

"And why is the Paragon on your tail?"

"You'll never guess what happened." Emily beckons him to follow her to a mini-daycare table and benches tucked into an alcove away from prying ears. Skyler can't help but remember that they were just kids not so long ago.

As it turns out, Emily invited herself to Adeline White's private party using Instructor Paradis's ticket left unattended on the classroom desk. Emily put on her mother's dress, ticket in hand, and went to the secret meeting place Emily had overheard while her teacher was in conversation with another guest. The Paragon agents, who were working overtime to guarantee some extra benefits for their families, did not question where her ticket came from or why she was unaccompanied.

She was then spotted by Kahlo White, one of Adeline's two sons, who has a crush on her. That's how she was recognized and how the officers chased her to the park. At least, that's her side of the story.

"No, no, no," Emily suddenly repeats, restless. "That's not possible."

"What?"

She doesn't answer right away, her eyes darting back and forth, then when they lock on him, Skyler can already sense trouble.

"This is a bad idea."

"You don't even know what I'm thinking!" she shouts. Then, scanning him from head to toe in her unique way, as if she could see something invisible, she adds, "You don't have to be so insecure, you know."

"Yes, because you are predictable in your unpredictability."

"I want you to know that this is for a good cause. Didn't you say earlier that I need a mentor? Don't you believe in my ability to prove what I can do?"

"I thought so until you illegally snuck into a secret party hosted by one of the most influential and ruthless people on the Ark. You have a knack for attracting the worst kind. There's nothing I can do to help you on this one."

Emily lets out one of her mischievous laughs that he dreads the most. Last time, he ended up trapped in a refrigerator of the dining hall with Chris Kay, a med student he avoids at all costs. It was simply because Emily wanted to get her hands on their waffle recipe, unable to accept the fact that they rarely offer them on their menu. She did try to coax them by saying it was a surprise for her sister Gabrielle's party, but Skyler knows it was an excuse to get an unlimited ration to satisfy her sweet tooth. He has learned the hard way not to get involved in her crazy stories unless he is willing to bear the scars.

"I need your help," she says, her words heavy with a meaning that does not bode well, and the pervasive refrigerant smell lingers in Skyler's memory.

"No. The risks are too great."

"Can you watch me wither away to death—my dreams shattered, forgotten, trampled to the horror of every art-knowing, life-affirming, beauty-loving mind the world has ever known? Not even you could afford the waste of a talent that honors our ancestors and our plans to repopulate the earth, restore meaning to our lives and—"

"What about my dreams of becoming a surgeon?"

"This will be the perfect opportunity to prove yourself! Think about it. This is exactly the game that's been played on this ship since the beginning of time. In fact, it's been played ever since the Flood washed away our planet, and only a handful of survivors, cherry-picked by the way, were rescued because they had the right connections."

"Sometimes I wonder if you are a mind reader." The thought of Emily patting him on the head with a Paragon power stick doesn't seem that far off.

"You are wasting your energy memorizing books that won't do you any good if you can't shine in front of the right people. You must socialize, even if you don't enjoy it. How many times have I told you that?"

"I hate that you're right," grumbles Skyler as he watches parents pick up their children.

"The truth can be hard to swallow, I know."

"Would you do the honors of clarifying the situation and how my help would make a real difference in your sorry mess?"

"When that damned Paragon found out my true identity, and I was forced to run away," she explains mysteriously, "I left my bag on the table by the buffet."

Of course. Emily couldn't resist dipping into the hors d'oeuvres.

"Your bag is officially gone forever," he argues, thinking about the sheer number of guests at the party and the safety hazard a forgotten bag can represent, especially from an intruder. "Forget about it. You'll be lucky if they don't press charges against you."

"You don't understand. My final assignment is inside my bag. Without it, I can kiss tomorrow's graduation goodbye. You wouldn't want to have to dance alone, would you?"

Not only would Emily then have to repeat the grade, but Skyler would no longer be able to escape the grips of an old arrangement between the Goldbergs and the Harrises. Emily was his way out of this would-be alliance between the two families. Except that if she can't graduate or accompany him tomorrow night, all his hopes would fall apart. He can't risk so much. Besides, isn't that what best friends do, support each other even in the worst of times? If he can't live up to their friendship, he's no better than those shallow people.

"I'll have my dad ask a colleague who works for Adeline White," Skyler suggests. "It'll have to wait until tomorrow, though. I'm sure you can work something out with Instructor Paradis, in the meantime."

"Why ask your father and potentially have my bag disappear forever when you can do it yourself? This project is my life!" she says.

Emily shrugs off Skyler's annoyed look and takes a deep breath.

"My reaching adulthood within the Ark depends on it," she blurts out. "There is a good chance that it's still untouched and in the same place. Adeline would no doubt blackmail your father or his friend for a trade. She would find out that it was my bag and go after my father and, of course, me as well. My father has suffered enough."

"Even if I accepted, I don't see how…"

Emily's expression changes dramatically.

"But if it isn't Edelsa Harris, daughter of the great Tom Harris, the timeless perfumer of the Ark!" she says with a fake smile.

Gaping, Skyler cranes his neck to see a girl emerge from the theater, opposite their alcove, and turn toward them as her freshly cut hair cascades.

"Bates," Edelsa hisses as she pulls up her turtleneck as if she could catch a cold by sticking around Emily.

"Skyler needs help."

He wants to kick her under the table, but he is no match for Emily's sharp reflexes. His toe meets the metal of the wall, and he bites his tongue while faking a smile to Edelsa whose confused look shifts to shock at warp speed.

"For the ceremony?"

"Even better," replies Emily, weighing in on every word.

"What could be better than the graduation ceremony with all the illustrious families of the ship and—"

"Adeline White's special soiree."

Edelsa gives a choked gasp, and for a moment Skyler thinks she's going to pass out. Her breathing finally stabilizes a beat later with a hand on her chest. Parents are glancing their way, and she edges closer to the alcove as if to hide. Her voice even, she says, "How could you possibly know such valuable information? Don't tell me your father managed to win Adeline's favor?"

"Not me, of course. Skyler was invited, but the idiot lost his precious ticket. Since it's the very first time he's been invited, he worries they'll turn him away at the entrance for his blunder. And he's quite self-conscious. So, I was thinking that if he could go with you … who is certainly one of their regular guests … It's really important for his future that he attends the party, you know, because of the mentorship tomorrow … you know what I mean…"

"Skyler," Edelsa says thoughtfully, her hand brushing Skyler's shoulder as he quivers. "Do you—"

He glares at Emily and remembers why their friendship has endured.

"If it's too embarrassing, don't worry about it. I don't want to push you," he replies.

"Of course not," she says in a sensible voice, very much in control of this absurd situation engineered by Emily. "It's true that they usually invite me to these parties, though I wasn't planning on going to tonight's, since graduation is tomorrow and all, but… I'd be really happy to help you."

She pauses for a moment and, in a tone that Skyler has trouble reading, she adds, "We also get to spend some time together."

The thing about Edelsa Harris is that there is nothing wrong about her. This sense of perfection is unsettling. Skyler embraces the imperfections that make people human, because that's what they are: poor, ever-evolving creatures who can learn from their mistakes and grow together; not frigid mirrors with flawless reflections to please. The chinks in their armor are what Skyler finds most attractive. He wants to stitch them up with even more beautiful pieces they can weave together through thick and thin. Otherwise, he'll never feel like he's enough.

"I'm going to rush to my cabin to get ready," Edelsa adds in a jerky voice. "I wouldn't want Adeline to think I'm not being serious about her evening."

"The party is already in full swing," says Emily, arms crossed. "It'll be too late by then."

"All right. I'll stick with the outfit I picked out especially for the play. Skyler?"

He suddenly becomes self-conscious in his old, worn-out Academy uniform. Why should he dress differently to spend time with his books? The flowers in the gardens don't care about these petty details either.

"I must have another uniform lying around somewhere," Skyler ventures.

"No time for that," Emily objects.

"She's right," says Edelsa. "I have just the right thing for you."

Despite his protests, Edelsa and Emily are working together —who would have thought?—to have him change in the Academy's furnished theater. The classrooms and medical labs are in the opposite wing, far from Emily's scrutinizing gaze and the faceless spectators in the empty rows of seats. His stomach lurches at this whole situation. Edelsa, on the other hand, looks ecstatic and totally in her element. She has stepped closer, so her hand accidentally brushes against his. When he realizes her move, she awkwardly steps aside and stands tall on her stilettos.

"A suited-up doctor on the eve of his graduation with an exquisite beauty from the ancient cities, on their way to a soiree full of the world's secrets. Convincing," says Emily.

"Shall we?" asks Edelsa beaming, her hand gravitating toward Skyler's arm.

He grunts his assent and steps off the stage first. Giddy, Emily darts toward him and whispers, "Isn't your entrance ticket pretty?"

3

Known for holding her parties in a private cabin, Adeline White decided to go big this time, refurbishing a section of the Ark that is now bathed in the illusion of a sea floor that keeps changing with the vibe. On display are ancient pieces, relics recently extracted from a particularly successful hunt. The surviving relics have been cleaned, but the ravages of time and water have damaged them to a point of no return. Fortunately, there are some technology and holographic reconstructions showing the difference between their current and original state, or so the Archives say.

No one pays them any real attention; everyone is too enraptured by the rare items on display and the chance encounters that break the overwhelming monotony of the ship. Glasses clink, hors d'oeuvres are served, and peals of laughter blend with the strange music of percussion and flutes.

The ease with which they were able to join this party has Skyler puzzled. Is this really all they need: a trusted name and a ridiculous outfit? As if that sort of thing is going to make a difference in this world that needs to be healed. It's hardly surprising that they're stuck at the bottom of the ocean if their ancestors behaved this way too, paying more attention to trivia than to the problems of this world.

As soon as Emily snuck away, Edelsa couldn't help but slip her arm under Skyler's. It was a matter of credibility, she assured him, but he knows that her gesture means more. The Goldbergs and the Harrises did everything they could to bring them together. They played along for several months, but Skyler couldn't keep up the charade. He never told Edelsa directly, but his silences and extended disappearances were his way of letting her know he wouldn't bow to the whims of their families who pander to the Ark's wheeling and dealing.

How could he possibly think of starting a family with a girl he barely knows and in such an unnatural way … while focusing all his energies on what really matters to him, which is medicine and requires endless hours of study? The others wouldn't approve—Chris, for example, who can be found flirting between two labs—but he sees no point in doing this, knowing full well that a superficial relationship would never lead to anything genuine. At best, he would have a child or two, their families would be happy, but behind the walls of their cabin, the sense of responsibility would replace the genuine connection that should bind two beings in the first place.

Edelsa's voice blends with the chatter around them with no need for Skyler to respond, his keeping quiet being a trait of his. They've been inside for a while now, but there are so many guests that they're struggling to reach the heart of the exhibit where, according to Emily, is the must-see centerpiece. The painting of a tanned, ageless man with a bewildered face who has been staring at him for nearly half an hour is starting to get on his nerves.

"Do you realize how lucky we are to be here right now? It's an honor reserved for a select few. Besides, I don't know why you are still friends with that Emily Bates. You deserve so much better."

When a pair of Deltas—they are easy to recognize with their small, black, and round glasses scrutinizing everything around them with their augmented vision—finally get out of their way, Skyler spots the buffet where Emily should have left her bag. He makes a show of going there, but Edelsa's hand pulls him back and he lets out a sigh of annoyance. So close.

"We just got here," she says. "I know you probably lied to me about needing to attend this party for your mentorship. I guess your friend needed a favor, but I didn't come here to make a fool of myself. You owe it to my reputation to behave properly."

"This evening should be enough to make you happy. You almost missed this wonderful exhibition."

"Yes, it is very unique, but that's not why I agreed to come, Skyler."

Her gentle eyes contradict her almost accusatory tone, and Skyler feels himself falter. For all the things he can accuse her of, Edelsa is anything but pretentious and dishonest. She is frank, and capable of making sensible decisions, except when it comes to more … personal stuff.

The rich, sweet, and heady smell that has been tantalizing him for a while finally overwhelms him. A flower comes to his mind, and he remembers the Harris perfumery, which is unique on this ship, the best place to forget the awful smell which soaks the ever-present steel walls.

"Jasmine?" he asks Edelsa, who is radiant.

"Only you could have such a sharp nose. I'm making my own brews in my biology class, and this is the one I'm using for my final project. Do you like it?"

"I love it. But I don't remember seeing jasmine in the gardens."

"My father has a private garden with hundreds of different flowers. If you ever feel like it, come visit. It would make him happy … and me."

Skyler resists the urge to say yes right away. She knows how to get under his skin, but he wouldn't want to give her the wrong impression.

"I'll think about it."

"The blooming should start in two weeks. That will be the perfect time before our mentorship begins."

He offers her a smile as he imagines what this piece of paradise must look like, but the consequences that his visit might bring leave a bitter taste. Their parents would never understand their friendship could go on without marriage. With Emily, it's different. Being a Bates, no one could imagine such a thing. They're right, but not for the right reasons.

Edelsa seems disappointed in his lack of enthusiasm, but Skyler can see that she is trying to stifle her disappointment by taking a deep breath. As if on cue, the guests scatter. Skyler takes this opportunity to reach the marble block that serves as a pedestal for the centerpiece, close to the buffet arranged near the back wall. Two men Skyler has seen before—at the Academy, maybe—are standing there. The one with the platinum blond dyed hair is noticeably taller than the second. Their discussion is lively, and Skyler steps away, unwilling to get involved.

The centerpiece is a gigantic celestial map on a stone disk with eroded pictorial inscriptions. How and why did the hunters manage to get it back to the Ark? While they should be focusing on locating food sources and lost technologies that would be useful to them, Adeline White has commissioned the recovery of this ancient object that must weigh a ton. Her ties to the Sigma Foundation must run deep to have been able to convince them. They could have simply collected digital data and added it to the Archives—which the Sigma Foundation runs —even if it meant showing a hologram for this soiree.

The inscriptions glow under the best lighting, which brings out the totemic reliefs. Skyler recognizes the sun, the moon, and a constellation or two, but his knowledge is limited. Hieroglyphic inscriptions give him a serious urge to go to the Archives to conduct his own research.

"The masterpiece of an ancient civilization whose shamans could predict the future and read people's thoughts," explains the guy from earlier, the smaller of the two. "They used mind-altering substances, but in their trance or psychotic episodes, they achieved unprecedented technological and artistic feats. They predicted the Flood with unparalleled accuracy. It is even suspected that the Founders settled in their village years before, and that these predictions inspired the creation of our Ark."

"Who were these people?" asks Skyler, intrigued by this story never told in their history classes.

"The name of this strange people has been lost through the ages, but they are called the Flaminis, because of the nature of their creations and their shamanic powers. These relics are the only remains that lead us to believe they were real."

"It's good to see you here, Kahlo," Edelsa says, deliberately ignoring the platinum-haired guy who just joined them.

"Larson didn't want to come, but our mother would have been furious," Kahlo says. Larson nods at them, clearly uncomfortable in this crowd.

"Do we know anything else about these Flaminis?" inquires Skyler.

"It is believed that these people waited too long for the fateful moment and that it killed them. There is a theory that the Founders of the Ark did live with the Flaminis, and that some of them lived among us, or at least their descendants."

In a corner of the star chart, Skyler notices sinister engravings that must represent this famous calamity that the Flaminis had predicted. Kneeling, people have their heads raised toward the sky where a kind of luminous radiation dazzles them. Strange rendition.

"Mother and her fancy ways," Larson complains. "As if we didn't have enough to deal with already." Skyler likes Larson right away. Few people admit their problems so openly and pragmatically.

"You don't understand what Adeline White has done for this ship," Edelsa replies stubbornly. "Without her, the Sigma Foundation would never have been able to expand the Archives, and we would be even more ignorant than we are about our own planet."

"Pieces of rock that weigh a ton and caricatures painted with gouache won't get us out of the Ark. If the Creator can be seduced by a contemporary art museum, we're really screwed."

"What exactly do you know about the Creator?"

"Why not take advantage of the art gallery?" suggests Kahlo in an obvious attempt to calm them down. "Representations of shamanic visions on large canvases should interest you, Elsa."

"We're just talking, aren't we?" says Larson with a honeyed voice, like coffee with too much milk.

"I didn't come here to have a philosophical debate with your narrow-minded head," Edelsa says.

"Of course not. However, I do have something to show you and … actually, I need your help. A biology problem. That should interest you."

Edelsa seems taken aback and her gaze waltzes from Kahlo to Skyler. With a hesitant voice, she asks, "Can't it wait?"

"I insist."

"It won't be long, I hope. I wouldn't want to miss the rest of the exhibition."

"If that's what you're worried about, I'm sure my mother can give you a private tour if I ask her. Isn't that right, Kal?"

"Of course," Kahlo replies with a warm smile. "You are Tom Harris's daughter after all. Our families have worked together for so long. I don't see why Mother would object." Edelsa beams upon hearing this and turns to Skyler with a sorry look on her face.

"See you later?"

"You know where to find me."

She seems satisfied with his answer and takes the arm Larson offers her. Skyler wishes he could have learned more about Larson's opinion of the ship, but they are already deep into the heart of the art gallery adjoining the centerpiece exhibit hall.

"Have you seen Emily by any chance?" asks Kahlo. "I lost sight of her earlier."

"She came?" says Skyler who feigns surprise as best he can.

"I was surprised to see her too. I know how much Mother wants to keep her exhibits secret, and the Bateses … well. My mother caught us talking and signaled to her guards to chase Emily out of here. I would like to apologize for Mother's unpredictable temperament."

"I'll tell her about it."

Skyler manages to make it to the buffet, followed by Kahlo, who tells him about the next day's graduation ceremony. Skyler responds absentmindedly while scanning over the heaps of desserts stacked on top of each other near the occupied armchairs; Emily's bag is nowhere in sight. When he asks Kahlo why there are so many guests, he says, "I wouldn't be surprised if some people were looking for the slightest opportunity to find crucial information on valuable objects or leads on some artworks."

Suddenly there are shouts from all sides. Plates and glasses fall on the carpet.

"What the hell is this party? A play? First the kid makes a spectacle of herself, and now this!"

"Please, calm down Mr. Yang," says Kahlo who flies over to offer him a glass of alcohol he snatches on the way.

"I understand your confusion, but—" says Adeline White, dressed in white and looking every bit like a stray snowflake from the gardens.

Her face drains when she finally looks down.

"Is there a doctor here? Make yourself useful for goodness' sake!" she cries out, looking away, as Kahlo flies over to her side to calm her down.

Skyler steps forward to see the source of the commotion: a woman has collapsed to the floor. Heat flushing his face, he waits for someone to volunteer—this is the kind of party doctors in Med Bay attend, right?—but no one volunteers. Is he really the only one with a background in medicine?

"So?" repeats Adeline White. Kahlo glances over at Skyler, and one by one the stares turn to him.

The unease creeps in as Skyler moves forward with an unsteady step. He kneels to get a better look at what caused the loss of consciousness. As he examines the victim, the panicked whispers pick up, "No way!"

"The Creator has spoken!"

"The last judgment has arrived!"

"My god, stigmata!"

The guests, who had crowded around Skyler and the unconscious woman, recoil in one fell swoop.

Blood drips profusely from the woman's palms—Anika according to the whispers—in two circular spots. Skyler removes her jacket and tries to staunch the wound with the fabric of his sleeves—so much for the garment borrowed from the play's costume designer, sorry Edelsa. The blood quickly soaks the fabric.

The voices grow around him: "She should not be in this state! Anika is a diver. She has received rigorous training."

"Exactly! They are abusing them! It's high time they reconsidered their ways."

Sweat beads on Skyler's forehead as he continues to press.

"I need help! Please, someone come and help me!" he shouts.

But no one is listening, blinded by their frenzy. They are talking about something strange the divers found during their last hunt, while the victim is bleeding to her death. Is this really the Ark? A rumor mill that values stories over its own people? Over life?

Anika's milky skin is chafed with marks from her wetsuit. Blood pools in her palms, and trickles down her hairline. Skyler has never seen anything like this, not even in his Academy classes. And his visits to the sanctuary date back. The stigmata are just stories buried in the Archives he's barely skimmed. What if the Creator was really trying to tell them something?

"Get the hell out of here, boy, and go get help. Let me take care of this."

The hard yet benevolent gaze of Mrs. Farrell—the priestess of the Ark dressed in her ceremonial tunic—snaps him out of his trance. She helps him up, then addresses the crowd in a voice charged with a power that commands respect and echoes the Farrells of the Embarkment.

"May the Creator be merciful to us! For His Voice can take many forms and many faces. Fear will only blind us and hide his Message. Let us pray, for redemption and clarity, for in prayer alone can we take refuge during this uncertain time."

4

"I NEED TO CHILL."

Emily has been in a tizzy ever since she picked up Skyler from Med Bay where diver Anika is under observation; the doctors probably administered a coagulant to make her stigmata heal, but the prognosis is still uncertain.

Meanwhile, the lights in the Ark have gone into dim mode, meaning that the last meal of the day in the dining hall is long over.

"Hold it together. I'm sure we'll find your bag tomorrow."

"Do you realize that this jeopardizes my graduation?"

In a remote corridor of the ship, Emily tries to open the door in front of them, but it remains stuck as if there was some technical problem.

"See? It's time to go back to our cabins," says Skyler, trying to calm her down. "Who knows? Tomorrow we might have a better chance."

"I don't want to waste this last night of freedom when I'm risking my mentorship and the only hope for a future on this hellish ship!"

When Emily is in this state, it's best to listen to her. He

knows she's not having an easy time and it's at times like this that she needs him.

"Okay, but you are coming to the ceremony tomorrow," Skyler insists.

"Who will want to see me?"

"Me."

"Edelsa will want to go with you anyway."

"This is not our agreement."

She sighs heavily.

"You know I'd do anything to help you Skyler, but without my project, I'm going to make a fool of myself."

"Let's find a way then. You do not usually give in so easily. You have always told me to persist, no matter what others think."

Despite the hardships, Emily has always held her head high, a quality that Skyler finds more than admirable. When she found out that no one could be trained as a Paragon agent, she asked her father to secretly teach her. When she was denied the opportunity to become a relic hunter, she devoted herself to the arts without ever flinching. When her family was put through the wringer, she bounced back. Such resilience is worthy of the utmost respect.

"I'm going to need your help," she says thoughtfully.

"Tell me what I should do."

She offers him a smile of gratitude.

"Give me a little more time to think about it, but I think I'm on to something," she says, waving her wristband near the reader. "Why the hell won't this door open?"

The hallway is not very busy at this time, and there is no chance of anyone coming to help them.

"This door is secured, right? The Sigmas do not give access to their facilities unless there is a good reason," Skyler points out. Every time he wants to consult the Archives, he must follow a strict protocol.

"No, it should be working. My father gave me access to make me feel better about not being able to swim with the divers. Besides, I don't understand why they turned me down at the time. They're overworked!"

"Look at the note."

A piece of paper, stained and wrinkled as if it had been dipped in a dubious substance, is taped in an odd angle near the door. It says, "This section is off limits due to a broken pipe." They will have to go through the warehouse.

"A nice walk to warm up," says Skyler encouragingly. "Perfect for coming up with a solution for your project."

"No," sighs Emily, wincing. "But you can answer my questions about Adeline White's party."

Skyler knew it was coming. He did not tell her what really happened during the evening, as he was still in shock. On their way to the warehouse, he gives an account of the events while providing her some specifics about the artworks that were on display. Emily is disappointed by the lack of details, but information about the famous celestial map and its origins seems to make her happy.

"Didn't you see it when you were there? You can't have missed it unless you went straight to the buffet."

"I have good manners, Sky. No, it's just that my thoughts were ... elsewhere."

"No matter. If it had not been for Mrs. Farrell, the guests would have questioned me, or worse, they might have tried to connect me to the whole divine mark thing, for all I know."

"Do they really think this is the Creator's work?" says Emily in disbelief as they come to a doorway larger than the others.

The sigma symbol looks like a sturdy E having a bad day, breaking into two halves when the door slides open.

"All I know is that this woman had some very unusual injuries," says Skyler, who steps in first.

"Did you say she was one of the relic-hunting divers? What

if she got injured with a tool? God knows that those sunken cities are filled with sharp-tipped objects. A misplaced metal rod or nail can do a lot of damage."

"If that had been the case, how could she have gone to that party? No. The marks were deep and went through her palms. It happened suddenly, and she didn't even have time to scream. Anyone would have reacted for far less."

They pass through a large, dark warehouse that reeks of the rotting ocean. At the end of each row, the glow of screens shines on the gigantic crates stacked on either side. The shadows they cast make it look as if the place was inhabited, and yet they are alone, or so it appears. At this hour, the divers have long returned from today's hunting, but they usually go to the dining hall to unwind with a drink, or soak in the pool. According to Emily, they keep a strict schedule to ward off grisly accidents that go unreported—Skyler checked—but haunt the department and make it difficult to hire recruits. Superstitions trouble people's minds, for lack of better entertainment. Any attempt to show them there is no danger outside the ship's walls is to deny death itself, just because it is invisible to the naked eye.

These stories tell that time does not flow the same way in the deep sea. The hunters engrave the names of each of their lost on a metal tablet: their numbers are so great that you need augmented vision glasses to make out all the names. Before each hunt, the hunters offer a prayer to all who have died or disappeared in the bowels of the Great Ocean, their way of buying themselves peace of mind for a safe hunt. They also pray to receive the Creator's benevolence, learn the secrets of the old land, and succeed in their hunt to help the Ark recover the remnants of a far more advanced civilization.

Skyler knows Emily had prepared diligently to take her admissions test, but unfortunately, the Academy was not interested in her extensive knowledge of superstitions and folkways among this reclusive community shunned by the rest of the ship. Emily believes their superstitions may hold some truth, and others didn't like it. How could a teen know so much about them? It's not like those relic hunters are getting any attention. The best way to get rid of a little girl with undue curiosity is to douse the embers before they ignite, which is exactly what they did.

"There could be some unusual explanation," Emily muses.

"Isn't the Creator's message a pretty unusual explanation to you? Imagine, the guests started talking about stigmata, and they got upset." Skyler can still remember how worked up they were with their fingers pointing at the collapsed diver.

"These Believers see signs in just about everything, dead or alive!"

Something stirs in the darkness of the warehouse. They stop dead in their tracks near a screen that glows dimly with the bright rotating Sigma symbol, making the shapeless blobs of crates writhe. Skyler must blink to steady his vision.

"Why are we here again?" he asks in an uncertain voice.

"Don't move."

Their nightly strolls in the dark corners of the ship are nothing new, but they've never run into anyone until now. Arching her back, Emily takes on a defensive stance that worries Skyler. She's tried to convince him to go to training sessions with her and her father before, but he's always refused, arguing that it wasn't his thing. Now he bitterly regrets it.

The inky blackness swallows up his best friend, and he heads for the stream of light. He has hardly taken two steps when he feels something behind him.

Emily?

In the light glow of a screen further on, a girl with a large bag slung over her shoulder looks back at him before vanishing into thin air.

"I didn't see anything, sorry," says Emily, startling him. "What?"

"A girl was right there."

"Where?"

"She's gone."

"Why didn't you scream?"

"I don't know! She took me by surprise. I thought it was you." Emily lets out another of her exasperated sighs and relaxes.

"Come before more show up," she says, taking his arm. "I wouldn't want you to be the victim of my sins."

"What do you mean by that?"

They walk through the rest of the warehouse across from where that strange girl was and emerge in a room with a gigantic pool, its light shimmering against the ripples caused by the Ark's hunter-divers taking turns swimming. Skyler may not be a born athlete, but these improvised swims always energize him. When was the last time they came?

"Never mind," Emily says as she squats down and dips her hand to test the water temperature. "Some nasty memories of bullies looking for fun."

"Emily…"

"Don't worry about it. It turned out all right," she replies, getting up. "It's time to relax!"

She leads him to the locker rooms, where they each go their separate way to put on clean bathing suits made available to the public. Although this pool is the divers' favorite place, any Archean can come. It is not as popular as it should be, as simulations are a better way to switch off during the little free time they can afford. But then again—apart from the mandatory quarterly simulations for everyone—having a gilded family is still a prerequisite to enjoy leisure simulations. The Goldbergs go occasionally, but often without Skyler, who does not see how an illusion will help them solve the current problems they are facing.

By the time he and Emily are standing on the pool deck in

their bathing suits, a dozen or so divers are doing their typical swims that involve competing against each other. They take turns swimming laps until one of them gives up, which can take a pretty long time. Skyler can't imagine how grueling that must be, while he barely manages a few laps that will leave him sore in his shoulders for the next two days.

"I should follow your workouts, just to stop hurting so much every time we come here," Skyler says, anticipating the next day's muscle hangover.

"We'd spend more time together and you'd know how to defend yourself," she replies with a wink. "Stop resisting!"

Before she can add anything, Skyler jumps in to get a head start on Emily, who is competitive as well, pretending to be a relic hunter herself. For now, Skyler must suffer to live up to her ambitions.

The water is cold today and the repetitive movements of his arms and legs keep his mind busy enough to forget Anika and her injuries. What will he do next time something like this happens? His classes at the Academy did not prepare him for anything like this. Without a mentor to train him properly, he will pale in comparison to Tamara Goldberg, and his family may lose some of their benefits.

He shakes off his worries by kicking the water more eagerly until he reaches the other side of the pool. Emily hasn't caught up with him yet, so he swims back. This would be the first time he could beat her. She always challenges him when she knows she can win, but he doesn't mind. He can get better every time, pushing beyond his limits, though Emily can get a little too intense sometimes.

Skyler slows down, his burning muscles a sore reminder of his lack of exercise, and he wished he could have enjoyed it longer. He lets himself float on his back to rest while staring at the light reflecting off the ceiling with the regular lapping of the water in the background. Emily still hasn't caught up with him after a while, so he dives to swim back to the edge more quickly.

When he emerges, panicked shouts erupt in a psychedelic swirl. The water has turned an all-too-familiar color: a crimson red whose strands are spilling like a ripped-out spider web.

Skyler swims toward the nearby group of divers trying to get out of the pool.

"What happened?" asks Skyler, who is helping them hoist injured divers as the blood spill expands in the water.

"This is the team from this morning," replies a rather tall diver beside him, one of the captains according to the star-shaped badge on his suit. "I knew they shouldn't have gone into the waters of Chaos."

Meanwhile, Emily lifts herself out of the pool, leaving a puddle of dirty water in her wake.

"Did something die in there or what?" she asks while rubbing her skin vigorously.

"A little help wouldn't hurt," says the captain, his face flush with exertion.

Emily winces at all the blood, then after taking a deep breath, helps them out, careful not to touch the blood.

"Sightings of the Leviathan have been reported more than once," the captain adds. "Every time the Ark sails through these waters, for that matter. The Creator has his reasons for steering us off course. Not that those big shots would care in the slightest about keeping us safe!"

"Don't be a fool!" interjects an older diver sitting nearby, her voice weakening as she clutches the towel Skyler gave her to staunch the blood. "If you believe in these sea monsters, you'll never be able to do what you're expected to do: hunt."

"So why did they keep the sonar and ocean current data from us? Clearly because there was something those blasted Deltas didn't want us to see. What right-minded soul would swim into the mouth of a monster?"

"Look at them! They had nothing until now! Can you see a monster in this pool? I surely can't."

"Only hooks could have cut through them so badly."

Getting involved in their discussion being the last thing he wants, Skyler walks away knowing that he would only make a fool of himself if he tried to treat these new victims.

"Alicia!" shouts the captain as he kneels beside his teammate who has just lost consciousness.

Skyler rushes to an emergency console for help, and he can barely hear the voice asking him to report the situation. All he can think about is that his medical skills did not prepare him for this. Useless. Again, the helplessness gnawing at him cannot explain or save these people passing out one after another.

"Skyler. There's nothing else you can do," Emily says after he cuts off the call.

She looks at him as if reading his mind. He lets out a laugh that rings hollow as it echoes against the tiled floor.

"Is that what a doctor would do, you think? Always defer to others and hope for the best? Or worse: close your eyes and forget that you can do anything?"

"Nobody knows what this thing is. Unless you are a miracle worker or a believer in the Creator's miracles, you just cannot save everyone."

Skyler will not tell her, but he knows his shortcomings. He will never be good enough. What would he do if Emily had these strange marks? There would be nothing he could do, and the same would happen all over again.

"Maybe you are right," he concedes, though the bitter taste of defeat lingers.

Waiting for help, the group of divers raises their voices as their teammates lie unconscious at their feet. Skyler and Emily exchange a worried look. Then, out of the blue, a trail of blood appears in the middle of the tile floor leading to the locker room, as if someone had dragged themselves across.

"I'm not sure I want to know where this leads," Emily says, stepping aside.

Fearful, they follow the trail, which gets thicker as they near the locker room.

A diver bearing the same marks as the others is slumped on all fours while moaning jerkily. But the details don't elude Skyler this time. His injuries are much more severe. Not only do the hands, the crown of the head, and the feet look like they have been pierced through, but a network of bluish filaments akin to blood vessels spreads out from the marks as if running through the bloodstream like a throbbing poison.

They recoil at the diver who gives them a bloodshot look.

"We shouldn't stay here," says Emily, her voice shaking.

5

"I KNEW THERE WAS SOME TRUTH TO THE LEGEND OF THE Leviathan!"

Emily is excited as ever, so much that her scream startles a tank-topped man painting a deck of cards on a dining table of the canteen. The pungent smell of paint wafts through the air as the contents of a can spill onto the floor. Skyler apologizes for Emily and offers to help him clean up, but the man pushes him away. Skyler doesn't wait a second longer and scurries down the hallway with Emily.

The last time Emily was so excited was when she wolfed down some leftovers Skyler had brought back from the fancy restaurant of the Ark. Skyler hates it whenever his family takes him there. They always steer the conversation to their idyllic past and the slippery slopes of tragic events that have befallen them. During these outings, Skyler always brings something to keep himself busy—in this case his homework—to tune out his parents and avoid their admonitions for failing them as a son.

"Didn't you say those stories about the Creator were nonsense?"

"The trick is to know what's real and what's not," Emily says lightly.

"How do you know this story is even true? With the sheer number of superstitions and myths out there, a hellish snake is the most far-fetched I have ever heard."

The Archives do speak of the Creator myth, but no direct scientific observations have ever been reported, or if they have, their data is incomplete and lost forever. It is not known how reliable and comprehensive those records are, but since it's their only source of knowledge about their ancestors, they have no choice but to rely on them. The Leviathan may be one of those stories that has slipped through the sands of time. Who knows what really lurks in the unchartered abyss of the Great Ocean?

"Even if it turned out to be fake, I'm sure there's enough truth to make up for my art project. It's the perfect source of inspiration."

"It's getting late," says Skyler, who does not feel like getting himself wrapped into baseless claims.

He should already be back in the family cabin, even if it is the last place he wants to spend the night. Tomorrow will be busy.

Once the graduation ceremony is over and his mentorship is official, he will be able to live in his own cabin. It will be modest, not to say abysmal, but it will be better than having to deal with his father's mood swings and the stench of a past he can never shake off. His future cabin will be what he has always wanted: a quiet space, his own world where the impossible can be challenged with no one to answer for. Hopes nurtured and dreams nourished by his garden that will bring him a little closer to the land of old and, who knows, a promising future if he can heal enough people on this ship. The Creator might even grant him the redemption he has so often hoped for.

"Skyler! You can't leave me now," Emily snaps, blocking his path.

"I have a bad feeling and we are already too involved."

They might get arrested in the middle of the graduation ceremony, which would confirm his family's suspicions about Emily's bad influence. He adds, "If the Paragon finds out about what we did, what would we tell them? Sorry we crashed Adeline White's private party twice, where a diver almost died on the spot. Sorry for going to the divers' pool, which, by the way, is off-limits that late at night. Coincidentally, as the diver team fell into unconsciousness, bleeding to death on the floor, we decided to run away instead of waiting for the Paragon to explain what happened. Quite the story!"

"You know very well why we didn't stay. I don't want to spend the last night of our childhood in a cell. However, it's not too late to make this night unforgettable."

"Isn't it memorable enough already?"

"Wait until you see the Leviathan with your own eyes. Our children and our children's children will talk about it, and our legend will travel the length and breadth of the ship. Those who found the Leviathan and saved the only Ark that survived the Flood from a tragic end."

Nothing can change Emily's mind now, but she is right about one thing: this is their last chance to roam the Ark's hallways, free of their obligations. The mere thought of having to raise a family with Edelsa Harris compels Skyler to put off his future as a responsible Archean for a while longer. If a mythical sea serpent decides to show up, it will make for an unusual story to tell. If people affected by the stigmata suddenly show up, this night could be oddly promising.

"Alright, you win. But just this once," Skyler drops, his heart pounding.

Since crashing into this private party, the sweet taste of adventure has been tickling him, even though he can smell trouble. But to be honest, he really can't see how things could get any worse.

"You're making me so proud," squeals Emily as she gives him a friendly hug, a rare gesture from her.

"Better enjoy it then," he replies, patting her on the back. "It is not going to happen again."

"Let the mission begin," she says theatrically.

BEARING the triple triangle of knowledge, the Delta laboratories coordinate the Scientific Wing that includes the oceanography and lost technologies, the Sacred Fire with all the ship's machinery, and finally the greenhouses that feeds them with fruits and vegetables, a welcome change from the seaweed and fish of the Great Ocean. This is the most complex and essential division of the Ark. It's all thanks to their know-how that they have been able to survive for so long.

As they shuffle down the corridor, Emily does not look so excited at the thought of meeting a legendary creature anymore, dummy or not. Or is she scheming to get back her art project she lost in Adeline White and her consortium's stronghold?

Tonight's chain of events does not bode well for them, and Skyler's anxiety is not going anywhere. The Paragon could lock them down in their cabins until they can solve the mystery revolving around the stigmata, which would in turn affect their graduation and mentorship. Not only that, but they would easily link those events to Skyler and Emily, who would then have to contend with a host of tricky questions that could get them into deep trouble. The Paragon will find a culprit, no matter the cost, if only to earn the Ark's trust in their unquestionable ability to keep them all safe. Under every commander, the Paragon has never failed, not even once. A bunch of teenagers directly or indirectly involved in some mysterious events could easily be used as scapegoats, just to keep their credibility as an elite force sworn to protect the passengers.

Sometimes Skyler wonders who or what exactly they are protecting: their reputation or their power base?

On their way to the oceanography section, thousands of plants in rows crowd the greenhouses which give off heat through the glass barrier, as if a miniature sun were walled in. The temperature sensors work well here, unlike the park choking under the artificial snow, where those Paragon agents must have melted by now, and hopefully their will to track them melted down along with it. Right, he had forgotten about them.

Monitoring the ventilation system is certainly not on top of the Deltas' to-do list, even though the gardens warrant the same level of attention. Some rare species of plants manage to squeeze through the undergrowth, though not always successfully. When the time comes to go back to the Surface, those plants will enjoy the natural sunlight, given they were taken care of in the first place.

"Do you think your father would know anything about what happened to the divers during their last hunt?"

"The question is whether he will cooperate. Make sure you do not talk about the Leviathan around him. My father hates anything related to pseudoscience." Emily chuckles, and Skyler gives her a questioning look.

"No wonder who you take after."

"That is not very nice of you," replies Skyler, annoyed.

"I love you too," she says, turning to face him with her arms spread wide. "Sorry for being so blunt with you, but until the Creator cleanses me with His light, I couldn't resist."

Suddenly, a door bursts open, and gas rushes out through a beam of sunlight.

"Is that what you call a sign?" says Skyler dismissively as he walks past her.

"I wish it were that simple."

Driven by curiosity, Skyler steps into the greenhouse and winces at the stench of plants mixed with ammonia. The plants all look the same at first glance, but he eventually recognizes a few: roses, chrysanthemums, hydrangeas. Other flowers from the park can be found a little further on, grouped by family, such as Asteraceae, orchids and more. A little piece of paradise.

He notices something strange at the base of the fruit-bearing shrubs where some weird seeds are nestled in the heart of dark purple flowers. Intrigued, he plucks one of them to smell its aroma, but it slips through his fingers.

"Look who I found!" shouts Emily, as she deftly overpowers a masked girl with an armlock.

The same girl Skyler caught in the Sigma hunter-divers' warehouse, stares back at him with a forbidding look. Skyler bends down to pick up the seeds that have fallen out of the flower, but the girl shouts angrily, "Don't touch them!"

"Why not?"

"With such a big batch, you'd fall into a very deep sleep like Sleeping Beauty, and perhaps you'd wake up if your prince could give you an antidote within ten minutes. Not to be the killjoy, but I don't see any prince around."

"I wouldn't be stupid enough to swallow them."

"You were going to smell them, weren't you?"

How would she know? Skyler rubs his hands against his uniform, his heart drumming against his chest.

"That's what these Arahmises do. They lure their victims with their enchanting gas and their seeds take care of the rest. They give off a gas that, once breathed, acts almost instantly."

"These things should not exist on this ship. Why keep them here?"

"In small doses, they can be useful for those who know how to use them."

"You mean it's a drug," cuts Emily.

"Who hasn't dreamed of a prince to come and rescue them?" The girl looks like she's about to laugh at them with her half-smile.

"I don't see what's so funny," retorts Skyler.

"Arahmis seeds have quite the reputation on the Ark, but bourgeois like you haven't taken a liking to them. Yet. Or maybe you missed the boat. Just your luck."

"Do you realize this drug could kill us?" he insists, still reeling from almost falling into its trap. "The health risks are too great for these flowers to be left in the open like this!"

"You're being the nice doctor now?" mocks the girl whose mask slips under her chin, showing a youthful face uncharacteristic of her attitude. "Not that I'm complaining about this souped-up version of the prince, but once in limbo, it takes more than a kiss to emerge."

"You've already had those seeds before," says Emily matter-of-factly. "You're a drug addict."

The girl seems caught off guard and bursts into a hearty laugh.

"You're not as dumb as you look. I like you." She sharply spins around and somehow breaks free of Emily's grip. Stunned, Emily watches the addict whirl awkwardly into some young trees that sway under the impact.

"Not that I don't enjoy your company, but I have work to do." She pulls out a half-filled glass bottle of seeds from her sling bag, slips the mask back over her nose, and goes back to harvesting, as if their presence was nothing more than a minor misunderstanding. Emily shrugs at Skyler's scowl, and he reaches for the bottle himself.

"I cannot let you do that," he says angrily, but the girl breaks away like a breeze.

"How are you going to stop me? I'm not dying of poisoning, so your doc skills are useless. At least your pretty girlfriend has figured out that you should let the grown-ups go about their noble business."

"Noble!?"

"Don't be a scaredy-cat. From your ivory tower, everything

seems so dark, but the truth is, you're only staring back at your own reflection." This girl speaks a language completely disconnected from reality. These seeds must have left debilitating damage to her neurological network.

"Give me that bottle. Now!"

"And what will you do with them? Sell them? I can't pass on this batch while the market is booming."

"I'll burn them."

"If the seeds burn, their toxic fumes will cause irreversible damage across the ship, spreading through the vent ducts, and sparing no one. I'm pretty sure that's not what you want. That is, unless you want to prove to everyone on this ship that you are the hero we need in times of chaos. Well, I hate to disappoint you, but I wouldn't stake such a high price on your heroic act. Maybe a kiss at most."

"The Paragon will know what to do with those seeds," he replies, annoyed, "and with you."

"More importantly, they'll have a fine suspect with a staggering amount of this fabled drug. Your choices are limited, Doc."

He pulls his hand away, as if the glass were burning hot, while Emily watches them intently. Why the hell isn't she helping him out? And how would this girl know he's a med student? They've never met before.

He stands still, his mind racing.

"That's what I thought," says the girl, while deftly filling her bottle, faster this time.

Numb with shame, Skyler hates himself for not thinking clearly. Can't he even stop her? Pathetic.

"It's an odd time to be walking around here," says a middle-aged man standing at the entrance to the greenhouse, while rubbing his stubbly chin.

The three gleaming silver rings he wears on his thumb, index and middle fingers give him an intimidating look. Such valuable jewelry is not a commodity on the ship, where its material would be more useful in making parts or any electronic equipment. Did he take advantage of his position with the Deltas to get his hands on those relics or is he one of those ruffians who insist on showing off?

"I need to see Dylan Goldberg. He's my father," says Skyler, who can't remember ever seeing the man at the labs in the past.

"Goldberg…" He pretends to check outside with a quick glance, but an evil smile creeps across his face. "He's not here," the man says, clinking his rings together.

"It's important," Emily adds, as surly as ever, intent on the man.

"And you are?"

Emily, who is usually quick on the draw, hesitates. If she admits she's a Bates, she could be in serious trouble, not to mention loitering in a greenhouse hiding an illegal mind-bending drug.

"A new friend," the addict cuts in casually.

"I wish you'd told me about your new friends before giving them a tour, Mara," he replies in a strained voice. "You should trust a limited number of people. You never know what's going on in their heads."

"I'm aware of that. However, I have no idea what the doc is doing here."

"I came to see my father!" Skyler retorts defensively, as the man gives him a menacing look.

"And broke into one of our greenhouses, while possibly contaminating it," the man says. "Since your father is not around, let me show you the way out."

"I'd better get going too," Emily adds. "We'll catch up later, Mara. Next time, I'd like to meet your family someplace less … awkward. I don't like making a bad impression."

Skyler and the man are both dumbfounded, but the latter quickly regains his composure, and gestures toward the exit.

Emily and Skyler are escorted out of Delta Labs and are met with an unsympathetic look every time they glance over their shoulder. And all the while, Mara the drug addict carries on with her illicit dealings.

Outrage flares inside Skyler as he stares at the ground on the way out.

$$6$$

Their steps echo in the ship quietly sinking into the arms of Morpheus. They do not cross anybody on their way to their respective cabins, with only silence and their thoughts for companions. Skyler's mind is buzzing.

"Why didn't you do something?" he says, stopping near the elevators. "You could have overpowered them both!"

"They were obviously in cahoots," Emily replies in an unnaturally calm voice. "Messing with the Paragon again is out of the question. I think we should look at the records in the Archives."

"I have had enough for tonight," says Skyler, pushing the elevator call button a little too hard.

"So, you want to give up now?"

"If it's to prove this underwater creature story—"

"The Leviathan."

"Yes, this Leviathan is not worth it. And clearly, I cannot do anything for those people affected by the stigmata. Tomorrow is graduation and the beginning of adulthood."

"All right."

Skyler expects her to add something, but she doesn't.

"Is that it?"

"Your pride has taken a toll with Mara and that man. I understand." Skyler is a bit puzzled: the Emily he knows would try anything to convince him to pursue this mission—that's the feeling he's had since the chase in the park anyway. He retorts, "I cannot have a clear conscience knowing that these demonic seeds," Emily laughs at this, "can fall in the hands of Archeans who will end up in Med Bay, or worse, die of an overdose. Imagine if a child came to—"

A baby crying nearby shuts him down. He rushes in that direction with the horrible feeling that something bad has happened. The barely upholstered chairs of the nursery are empty at this hour, though a strong smell of baby powder and disinfectant blend in a strange cocktail.

Still dressed in his formal attire, Kahlo White is sitting by the entrance, cradling a red-haired baby. Emily's eyes sparkle as she listens to him reciting a children's story.

> *"In an emerald sea, a smirking fairy*
> *Met a tawny child, with a golden smile*
> *She was a sight to behold, full of promises untold*
> *So he crossed the line, to meet the divine."*

It's the opening verses of the legend of the Fairies, a grim hundred-year-old children's story that has gone through many changes, but this is the version told to every child on the Ark. It is neither good nor bad, and its contents can be interpreted in many ways. Some see it as a story to protect children from their innocence, and others, like some of the more extreme Believers, read it as the Creator teaching his Dark Ways.

Legend has it that one morning, a Fairy appeared to a young boy. She promises adventures and wondrous worlds beyond the walls of his village. The boy, having only heard of the world outside, is mesmerized and lured into the Fairy's clutches. Naturally, she becomes the best friend he has always dreamed of, and every now and then, she shares with him a little more of the world she comes from—its titanic waterfalls, crystal forests, endless starry skies, and exotic food with the power to give the clairvoyance of a seer or the courage of a hero.

But living in this idyllic world comes at a price, there are trials to overcome. Only those who are brave, wise, and powerful enough can hope to stay and explore its wilderness. The boy assures her that he has all these qualities and that he will learn if necessary. His teachers say he is a fast learner, after all. The Fairy promises to help him, and he trusts her. That is his biggest mistake.

Bound by their friendship, the Fairy shows him more and more fragments of her world overlapping with his, while testing his resilience. One night, when she feels he is ready, they cross the barrier that separates their two worlds, and it is incredibly painful. The ether is so dense that it poisons the mind. Once the boy is in the Fairy's world, his dreams become an endless stream of ghastly nightmares, so much so that he becomes gravely ill.

As long as he stays, he loses himself until he becomes a shadow wedged between two worlds, a sigh of silent agony.

While the disease is crippling him, the Fairy takes over the body of the young boy that remained in his home world, to carry out her evil plan: to sabotage the human world. By the time the boy realizes this, it is already too late. There is no way back. The rushing of the waterfall and the tinkling crystal leaves of the dreaming trees drown his screams of terror.

Stranded in the Fairy world, the boy sets on tackling the trials, since the Fairy left him to his own devices. But where is she? Didn't she promise to give her unconditional help? The ache of having been betrayed burning in his throat, he cautiously befriends other boys and girls who have fallen prey to the Fairies' charms, for thousands of them—no, an army—are invading the human world to conquer it. But there's something they hadn't thought of, a fundamental rule that comes with crossing over: a body for a body. A mind for a mind. For as many Fairies that have infiltrated Earth, there are as many children who can fight them off living in their fake idyllic world.

Together, the children succeed in breaking through the ether barrier and ousting the Fairies from their minds. They defy the odds by becoming the heroes of their own story, mastering the knowledge of this strange world, and aborting the prophecy foreboding the decline of the human world.

The boy returns to his village, having learned the true value of friendship and the importance of trust. But his world is not what it used to be.

The story ends here for children, but an extended version exists in the Archives, and it's not pretty. When Skyler stumbled upon it, he had nightmares about it for days. This tale that is supposed to be uplifting and teach important values gets completely turned on its head.

The origin of the Fairies remains a mystery in the original version, but the full version states that they are demonic messengers banished by the Creator. They are beings endowed with the breath of the Almighty who have misused their gift. The idyllic world described is only the flipside of their true lair. They are said to live in caves deep in the bowels of the Earth, where underground rivers flow and feed dark jungles whose roots support the world above.

There were not two worlds. There was only one.

They were cousins to humans—sharing the same planet—children of the same Creator, but they had chosen a different path, the wrong path, and they had been punished by the Creator who banished them from the rest of the world with a powerful barrier.

And they shine. Like fireflies, the Fairies shine in dark places.

It is said that the Flood is the Creator's means to banish

humans in the same way the Fairies were sent to the abyss because they strayed from the Great Design.

The Ark is stranded, not in a fiery hell burning with eternal flames, but in a cage of darkness sitting on the bottom of the ocean.

There is no way out.

They can only hope they were wrong. Yet Skyler fears that their possible salvation might be long gone. If these Fairies really exist, or at least their equivalent, there is no indication that they ever escaped.

Once the Creator's judgment falls, it is too late.

"This one's an illegal," Kahlo explains halfway through his story, the baby already asleep against his chest. "My brother had been taking care of him until Mother found out his secret. Well, our secret. Maybe I shouldn't have covered it up for weeks, but hey, with a little time, Mother will probably come around."

This child does not have parents? Unless they passed away, this is very unusual. Every family treasures its right to have two children. If an infant death happens, for example, there is no guarantee Command will grant approval to have children again. Since the Furies, the rules on the Ark have become stricter, and mistakes are punishable.

"You did the right thing," says Skyler, swallowing hard.

"It's not like you to put up with this kind of illegal act, let alone keep such a secret," Emily notes. "Are you all right, Skyler?"

"You're not going to tell the Paragon, are you?" snaps Kahlo. "That would be—"

"That's what I'm wondering," says Emily, crossing her arms.

"I'm not stupid," says Skyler, who hardens. "This child needs a family to love him. Not an army willing to get rid of him in the name of silly rules."

Emily gapes in surprise, and Kahlo relaxes.

"Hopefully, the people at the nursery will find a family for him," Kahlo says, kissing the baby's forehead.

"This place is not safe," Skyler replies. "The Paragon inspects all comings and goings. They will find the child. Take him to the sanctuary and tell Mrs. Farrell I sent you. She'll know what to do." The old lady can be trusted like no other person on this ship can.

"You think so?" asks Kahlo candidly. Emily gives Skyler an interested look and smiles, "If Skyler says so."

"Do not linger," Skyler insists, recalling the events of the evening. "Paragon agents could be combing the ship to get to the bottom of those stigmata."

Kahlo reaches over to an object beside the chair and hands it to Emily as he stands up, the baby against his chest.

"I believe this is yours."

"My bag!" she squeals loud enough to make the baby flinch in his sleep.

She opens it eagerly. Nothing seems to be missing given the broad smile that stretches across her face. She closes the bag tightly and presses it against her heart theatrically, "Kahlo White, you're my savior. Let me know if I can help you with anything. I insist, my dear."

Kahlo blushes and says, "Will you give me some time to think about it? Skyler's right. The sanctuary is the best place to go before things get messy."

"The baby!"

Some nasty crimson spots have appeared on the pearly cloth swaddling the baby. Kahlo's whole body is shaking, and sweat is running down his face frozen in terror.

"My hands," he mutters.

Black bruises cannibalize his skin, and from his palms leaks a darker-than-usual liquid, as if the blood was trying to clot. Stigmata.

But the word hanging on Skyler's lips is contagion. The

Whites were not among the divers, and none of them are supposed to have touched the victim at the party, at least as far as he knows. Could it be some kind of flesh-eating bacteria festering an open wound? Or was the seafood from the buffet contaminated?

"We're taking you to Med Bay," says Skyler, fear creeping. "Can you walk?"

"I think so, but my heart is racing."

"If you feel faint, lean against us. No direct skin contact. Better be safe."

Skyler can read the terror veiling Kahlo's gaze, but thankfully, Emily keeps her composure as if she had been trained to respond to this sort of crisis. Skyler grabs a fresh towel to take the child from Kahlo's arms. The little one could use some care too, with this strange disease running around, but the chances of him being found to be illegal are too great. If that's the case, he won't live another day.

Emily puts an arm around Kahlo's waist, then they run out of the nursery with dread.

"Who was the last person you had contact with?" asks Skyler urgently.

"I was with my brother Lars. He gave me the baby."

"Did you touch anyone else? The divers?"

"No, no. But you must tell my brother about the child. He entrusted him to me and—"

"We're on it."

Emily brings Kahlo to Med Bay, leaving Skyler in the adjacent corridor, away from prying eyes. An apple of life gently sleeps in his arms, and it is the most beautiful feeling he has ever known.

7

THE BABY SLEEPS SOUNDLY, OBLIVIOUS TO THE COMMOTION around him, as they arrive near the sanctuary where candles are floating in the darkness, while casting specks of light on the Believers' wrinkled faces. The place is more crowded than usual tonight. In these uncertain times, praying might be their only refuge. As Mrs. Farrell's warm voice helps them commune with the Creator, a torrent of childhood memories floods Skyler.

His family used to come here regularly when he was younger, and the stories the Farrells—who oversaw the sanctuary—told, filled his mind with possibilities. What if they lived on the Surface, what would it look like? What if the Flood had never happened, what kind of world would Skyler have grown up in? In these stories, there were three recurring characters, children, who would always get their feet wet, but each time, the Creator taught them a lesson on how to atone for man's sins.

The way Mrs. Farrell told her stories sounded as if these children had existed in time immemorial. As Skyler grew older, he wondered if these were stories that she had experienced herself, or whether the characters were her grandchildren. This wise lady would brush away a tear every now and then, though she would blame her clogged censer, her poor-quality sage, or the faulty ventilation. Skyler sensed that her memories were taking her back to a time far different from theirs. What had she experienced? Skyler always wondered, aware that his short life on the Ark could not replace a lifetime of experiences, nor could he come close to understanding its intricacies.

A long journey like Mrs. Farrell's is an unusual thing. The survivors she has met and connected with the Creator are as plentiful as the leaves on the trees in the gardens. She has lived a meaningful life that Skyler envies in many ways. Once, he thought Mrs. Farrell had lived through the Embarkment given her surprisingly accurate depiction of their ancestors' every word. It is a shame that the Goldbergs put an end to their visits to the sanctuary when their faith was shattered. But at bedtime and in his darkest moments, these stories live on in Skyler's mind, giving him hope that things can change for the better.

Skyler can feel the child's heart beating against his chest, and a soft warmth radiating from him. The most delicate and human thing there is—he can't just leave him.

Emily stayed at Med Bay to look after Kahlo. They agreed to meet up later, once Kahlo's condition is stable and the child is safe.

As Mrs. Farrell delivers the last words of her sermon, Skyler quietly walks into the sanctuary. Despite the darkness, she immediately locks her gaze on the child.

She glides toward Skyler in the quiet rustle of her priestess gown embroidered with gold and deep blue patterns. The glow of the candlelight reveals a series of symbols and drawings straight out of the same stories she tells the Believers. When she reaches him, she whispers, "Follow me, my boy." With a firm grip, Mrs. Farrell leads him down an adjoining corridor that opens into a shed, which makes a beeping sound at the touch of her wristband.

"Those damned devil leashes," she grumbles, seeping in a

rich cloud of incense that stuns Skyler but doesn't bother the child somehow.

Endless rows of shelves with stacks of jars filled with dried plants and two good-sized censers line the walls. Before Skyler can smell the contents, Mrs. Farrell sinks her hand into a small pile of dried leaves from a large, half-filled glass container, places them in one of the censers, and repeats the process three times.

"Let me tell you, sometimes I wonder why the Creator would bother with these jerks."

"You don't believe the stigmata are one of His messages?"

"Any more nonsense from you? He hasn't cared much about us in a long time."

"Doesn't the Flood refute that?" The Creator's ultimate answer to their ignorance: only knowledge and time can bring them their hoped-for redemption to return to where they came from.

"Boy, it's not that simple. There are worse things in this world. But this poor child is still pure and innocent," she says, gesturing to the little one stirring in Skyler's arms. "The last thing I want is haunting his nights with dreadful nightmares. Once they creep into our minds, they plague our poor souls ruthlessly."

"I was hoping you could help me." She stirs her well-filled censer and shuts the shaky door.

"Privacy is a luxury on this ship," she says, looking at the boy before sitting on a stool, her once humble posture subject to the vagaries of age. "An illegal, am I right?"

"How do you know?"

"You have no idea. I've seen others like him before."

Her face is veiled with sadness, and her voice is weary as if she had seen the same story unfolding before her eyes more often than she can count.

Mrs. Farrell stares at the floor, her hands resting on her lap, as she bites her lower lip. Skyler gives her the little one to hold, and her eyes turn glassy.

"Not even an ounce of respect," she breathes as she cradles the baby with trembling hands. "There were so many of them."

Skyler expects to learn more about them, but Mrs. Farrell is a treasure chest that knows how to keep her secrets safe from the most ardent thief. It's a technique she must have perfected over the years.

"There must be someone among the Believers who could make an exception," she mumbles in a hoarse voice. "I'll see what I can do. Who found him?"

"The Whites."

"Kahlo, isn't it? His mother thinks she's on a cruise ship, along with her wealthy people's club thrilled by the glinting of a piece of rock, or an odd stain! She won't even take my grandson's paintings because she's only interested in millennia-old works of historic value. Let's face it, they've all been drowned and buried since…"

Skyler lets her rant fervently, but he can't hide his discomfort. When she realizes this, she says, "No, but let's call things by their names! They are harmful to the Ark!"

"To get back to your question, Larson White found it." She grunts, all traces of sorrow gone.

"The scientist stuck in his lab? His madness for things too small to be disturbed will get the better of him one of these days. Why would the Creator have endowed us with microscopic vision if it's none of our business? We have enough problems to deal with without having to meddle in other people's problems, too."

"It's getting late," says Skyler, stepping toward the exit so he will not have to stay here all night. "I must go now. Are you sure there won't be any problem?"

"Most of these Believers are a bit fanatical, but not all of them. At least, they can be helpful if asked properly. Some incense should clear their heads."

Skyler doesn't know if Mrs. Farrell's smile is directed at him, but he smiles back out of politeness.

"Will you let me know about the child? I'm sure Larson and his brother will want to see him again."

"That I cannot guarantee, my boy, but the Creator will find his Way to let them know. He always does."

"WHY CAN'T Larson stay in his cabin like everybody else?"

The Delta Labs' doors loom up ahead, along with the vivid memory of their earlier run-in. Even the triple triangles seem to pulse with annoyance.

"I don't like it any more than you do," Skyler replies to Emily, who is fidgeting with the hem of her uniform. "But he has a right to know."

"What if we run into them again?"

"I prefer not to think about it."

Confronting the man showing off with those rings and the drug addict is one thing but turning a blind eye to their misdeeds is another. Being an accomplice is serious. Skyler doesn't even want to think about the consequences, but one thing for sure is that he would have to say goodbye to his dream, should any connection between him and the Arahmis seeds be discovered.

Her enthusiasm left in Med Bay, Emily takes the lead.

"I don't intend to spend all night here," she says without turning around. "Let's finish this job and get out of here. I sure need a good night's sleep."

Skyler hurries to keep up with her.

"Are you giving up your mission?"

"Giving up sounds a little too harsh to my ears, like one of those horrible screeching cats. We just need to catch our breaths. Who knows? I might wake up with my hands dripping in blood tomorrow morning."

Emily never fails to mention her aversion to cats when she gets the chance. Not that there has ever been a live cat on the ship, but about ten years ago, some students had some fun with a hologram from their animal biology class they had managed to hack into. It seemed like a joke at first; hundreds of cats swarmed every corner of the Academy for days. They would chase anyone who passed them, meowing and purring, until they became aggressive one day, hissing and lashing about with their sharp-clawed paws, and attacking anyone who got too close to them.

The hackers were found, and the holograms were disabled, but the damage had been done; hundreds of children, including Emily, suffered trauma from those fur balls. Skyler wasn't. If anything, he wanted to study them, so he and his brother spent a ridiculous amount of time trying to get close to them with no luck. The pets were too fast and hid behind the shaky metal-tiled walls.

"No kidding," says Emily as she slows down her pace. "I want to get to the bottom of this Leviathan mystery, but now that I have my art project back—bless Kahlo White!—I can have some peace of mind for a couple of hours."

"I didn't think you would give up so easily," Skyler says with a worried glance toward the greenhouses. "Any idea where Larson might be?"

"That way," she says as if it were the most natural thing in the world.

Skyler looks at her expectantly.

"What? I may be a Bates, but I know stuff."

"How long have you been seeing the Whites?"

"I'm not dating. I fraternize with the enemy."

She winks at him and steps into the next passageway that

loops around the Delta Department, away from the greenhouses, where all the private labs, and those the Academy uses for its science students, are clustered. Matching metal doors blend into a dim blur as they walk across, losing track of time and space. There's no way to know if the labs are busy, but with the coming graduation and the late hour, most of them must be empty or nearly so.

"His lab should be … here," Emily says, heading straight for a door kept ajar, the first since they stepped into this endless hallway.

A redheaded girl comes out at the same time, apologizes for bumping into Emily, then rushes out before either of them can react. Emily mumbles a snarky comment, then casually enters the White's lab. Skyler follows along and catches a whiff of fresh aromas with an undertone of acrid chemicals.

"You know it'll have to wait until tomorrow," Larson says in a charming voice with his back to the door. "I can't give you everything on the same night."

"Save your saucy remarks for the right person at least," says Emily. "If only your mother knew what you do when her back is turned."

"My mother doesn't care much about me, unless her reputation is at stake," he retorts as he turns around. He does not show a hint of surprise to find them in his lab.

"You have a way with words, I'll give you that, but will it be enough to ease Adeline White's torment about her wayward heir?"

Larson puts down the bottle he was examining with interest, then smirks at them.

"Either my brother is stupid, or he is intentionally letting the wrong people fool him. Sometimes, I just can't help but wonder whether he's stupid."

"Kahlo has always been nice and rational, unlike some people."

Larson has a frank laugh that rings like broken glass against the array of plants and foliage covering the walls, so it's impossible to see the true extent of his workspace. This lab looks very spacious by the sheer amount of equipment.

He rubs his face, as if he couldn't believe his ears.

"Are you going to tell me if the child is safe, or would you rather keep playing this tiring and frankly childish game?"

"If only it were a game," Emily replies without blinking.

"If you want to take over my mother's place on my list of the most annoying people on this ship, be my guest. Your name's climbing at lightning speed."

"The child is at the sanctuary with the priestess," Skyler cuts in, arms crossed, with an annoyed look at Emily who ignores him.

"The priestess?" Larson says, suddenly losing interest in Emily. "Why her?"

"She's the only person I trust. Better than the nursery where we found your brother."

"I told him not to! That's Kahlo all over again. Sometimes I wonder if Mother's naming him after a painting made him prone to seeking attention every chance he gets."

"He was named after a famous painter, not a painting," Emily corrects him in a deceptively scholarly tone.

"Never mind," Larson replies, sweeping the air with the back of his hand. "Now that that's settled, we can get down to business."

"And this is where our job ends," Emily concludes as she steps through the doorway. "You coming, Skyler?"

In the meantime, Skyler got distracted by a plant running up the walls, its buds about to bloom. This led him to the other end of the lab, which is disproportionately large, much larger than he thought. Vials filled with liquids of various colors are bubbling on wear-bleached metal counters, and white-powder-filled tubes piled on top of each other in the back. Immediately, the Arahmis seeds come to his mind, and he turns to Larson, "What kind of drug is it?"

"Do you really think I would produce drugs in my mother's lab? Way too risky, but I appreciate your keen observation. This powder should be my successful act of rebellion, right under her nose."

Skyler frowns and turns his attention back to the strange substance sleeping in crates that look suspiciously like those in the relic hunters' warehouse—the very place where Mara the drug addict was earlier. But was it really her? She was wearing a mask in the greenhouse, and the brightness was working against her in the warehouse. Maybe his brain made a false association, like when you meet a stranger that you think you know, until the moment you come closer.

"If you're so curious about my discovery, I can prepare a tasting just for you," Larson says, coming to stand beside him, with a pungent whiff of men's cologne. "Your friend as well, of course. I'm told it tastes like the dried seaweed in the shrimp rolls they serve in the dining hall."

"You mean you give out this homemade concoction? Without authorization?"

"They are willing people, believe me. I don't force them to do anything, but when you're hungry, anything will do."

"You can't," says Skyler, who feels sick to his stomach.

He has the same sinking feeling as when they stumbled upon the Arahmis seeds in the Deltas' greenhouse. The Ark's system already supports their basic needs. Why would they want to do things differently while endangering others? Short of sickly narcissism, Skyler doesn't see the benefit, especially given the workload involved. There isn't even a monetary system on the ship, as there was on the Surface prior to the Flood. There is a reason behind this. The evil that this system had caused was repeated so often in their classes at the Academy. Humans were drowning in their greed before they even enjoyed their earnings.

"At least I'm trying to make a difference on this ship," Larson says with a hint of tension in his voice. "I've heard of you. Skyler Goldberg, medical student, son of Dylan Goldberg, an oceanographer, and Murielle Goldberg, a nurse who was removed from duty for … what was it again?"

"Just drop it," says Skyler, who is boiling at the smug look on Larson's face, who is like a cat toying with its prey.

"Fine. I know you can't hold a scalpel without shaking to tears. That happened in your biology class, didn't it? Not your finest hour. Especially for someone intent on becoming a surgeon."

"Why is this even relevant? Why does it matter to you?"

"I don't question your goodwill, but it won't be enough. People talk. Your dreams are worthless if you can't do what's expected of a doctor."

Skyler had hoped this incident hadn't gotten out, but he had been foolish. The Ark does not forgive mistakes.

"Why should I listen to someone who deals in an illicit powder for people clueless about the risks?" retorts Skyler, clenching his jaws.

"There you go!" shouts Larson, rubbing his hands together. "You two are exactly the people I need for an extraordinary mission: a golden opportunity to keep reality from shattering your dreams."

"What makes you think we don't have better things to do, Larson White?" asks Emily angrily, stamping her foot on the lab door as if an invisible barrier was standing between Larson's world and hers.

"At my mother's soiree, I saw what you are capable of, Emily. Your dirty trick worked wonders on my mother and her lackeys who were too stupid to realize it was you. To be frank, I didn't think you'd have the nerve. You know how easy it would be to report you to the Paragon. But, of course, I can convince my mother to overlook this minor incident."

"What did you do, Emily?" asks Skyler, biting his tongue.

"Nothing serious," she dodges. Emily steps back into the lab, glancing toward the door as if she feared it would shut them in.

"If they don't comply with my wishes, you can talk them into it," Larson adds once she's joined them.

"Who are they?"

"The traders. The black market."

"Like I said, drugs," Skyler repeats, glaring at the powder.

"No, no, no. This powder has the power to change every-thing. How many illegals do you think are on this ship? Have you ever seriously given it a thought?"

"They dispose of them at birth. That's what they do," Skyler replies, bitterly. In the birthing department, he got a glimpse of this "compartment zero," the place where babies who go in never go out. It's a practice that happens all too often.

"Not all of them," Larson corrects. "Despite the Paragon's aura of supremacy, they are not foolproof. No one is."

His nonchalance is disconcerting. Can living in one of the most influential families silence the Command watchdog? Why does Skyler feel like it is virtually impossible to save those illegal babies through conventional means? The compartment is deadlocked, and every birth is catalogued by Med Bay, legal and illegal. No one escapes the Paragon's watchful eye.

Skyler doesn't understand why illegal babies are considered dead weight the Ark won't deal with. It's an inhuman system that doesn't consider life, only numbers and statistics.

"What exactly do you want us to do with this powder?"

"Whatever it is, we're out," Emily retorts, fear in her voice. "Let's go."

Larson chuckles, with a white-toothed smile as bright as his platinum hair. He has to live up to his family name, after all.

"What if the reward for helping me was … my brother? In

addition to convincing my mother to forget your scene at her soiree."

"I can date him on my own just fine, thank you," she retorts, but Skyler can see she's worried about her wrongdoing.

"All right, all right. But my mom's guaranteed mentorship, on the other hand, isn't a game you can win by yourself, is it?"

"She'd never take me."

"Despite Adeline White's regal demeanor, she'd do anything to keep my mouth shut about … shady matters. A mentorship is a minor trade-off for retaining her authority over humanity's last survivors."

Emily withdraws into silence, looking conflicted.

"As for you, Skyler Goldberg, I can't give you your most cherished dream, but I can give you the tools to make it happen. This lab will no longer be of use to me after this last task, which means you can use it as you wish. In order to match Tamara Goldberg, you'll have to be very creative and put on a hell of a show, though I suggest you leave the scalpel out of it."

"We don't even know what you want us to do with this powder and those traders," replies Skyler, who can't help but be tempted, not only by all the plants in this lab, but also by the facilities that outmatch that of the Academy in both quantity and quality.

The projects he has been mulling over for the past few years could see the light of day, even if Med Bay doesn't take him in because of his rookie mistakes.

"You must first promise not to disclose anything to anyone."

"We'll talk about it tomorrow, then," says Emily.

"Tonight."

"What's this?" asks Skyler as he continues to explore this fascinating lab. Ivy foliage is clumped on the glass walls of an inner chamber, as if attracted to it.

"Not that way," Larson says, grabbing Skyler's wrist with a hand covered by a strange glove that makes a clicking sound.

A rush of electricity runs through Skyler's body instantly. Dizzy, his vision splits momentarily. When he comes to his senses, Emily is about to incapacitate Larson with a blow.

"Easy," he says, holding up his hands. "After years of research, I can't risk leaking information about my experiments. The question now is not whether you will accept my request, but whether you want to be stuck here or help me as discussed. Am I clear?"

"I didn't see anything," Skyler says, feeling the muscles in his arm twitching.

"I'll make sure of that later. For now, there are more urgent matters worthy of your talents."

"Where did you learn your little magic tricks, Larson? You're playing with fire by taking Skyler hostage. My father will send a squad from the Paragon to seize the lab and stop the experiments you're conducting in secret."

"The Paragon is the least of my worries. You go on ahead, while I have a chat with Skyler. You have too much to lose to even think you can turn down my noble proposal. Are you ready to listen to me now, or are you so keen to challenge my family?"

A silence hovers with the popping sound of the beakers boiling over.

"Larson White," Emily growls, "you'll pay dearly for this."

"I sure hope so. Skyler?"

Skyler's eyes are fixed on the piece of metal lodged into his wrist, a technology he knows nothing about. Larson's apparent genius allowed him to not only tame these plants, but creep into the recesses of their lives. Skyler has never shared any of his plans with anyone, not even Emily. Yet Larson is right. Is this the real power held by the Whites?

"What are you hiding?"

8

"I can't believe we're risking our future for this."

"How many lives do you think are at stake?" replies Skyler, heart racing.

"We've been fooled by a rich kid playing with toys he doesn't understand himself. And to top it all, he had to spray his ridiculous cologne on us!"

Their mission is both simple and complex: to stop the distribution of a product on the Ark's black market, which is the only safe way to reach a group of illegals able to avoid the Paragon's sight. To ensure they stay healthy, Larson White created a formula to meet the basic nutritional needs of those children. While it is an imperfect solution, it will change the infant mortality rate among the Ark's castaways who have no access to proper nutrition. And during all this time, Skyler and Emily have been completely unaware of them.

Emily doubts Larson is telling the truth, but Skyler is inclined to believe him. When he turned the child over to Mrs. Farrell at the sanctuary, she was anything but surprised. Her help had already been requested for such a thing before. He would never know how many castaways had sought her out, but if he can help them in his own way, he will. Better than turning a blind eye on the ship's problems while leading a carefree life among the rest of the passengers, oblivious to what these children born at the wrong time must go through. How can he sleep after tasting the fruit of this bitter knowledge?

"And of course, this place has to be in the middle of nowhere!" Emily adds mockingly. "I'd never heard of locker sixty-seven before, have you? It sounds like a cheap dish in the dining hall."

"It's bay seventy-seven, not sixty-seven," Skyler chides her, glancing at the panels scrolling as they walk over a pair of wide doors, heavy enough to lock up a wild beast.

Funny how Emily's imagination about the Leviathan is infecting her mind with nonsense. If this thing were on the ship, they would know. People would talk, the Paragon would get involved, and anyway, what would be the point of having such a creature on board?

The strange stigmata must be caused by some type of bacteria—not by a legendary sea serpent.

Not quite sure if his skin came into contact with any of the infected people, Skyler reflexively rubs his hands together. Perhaps the bacteria can only be transmitted through touching an open wound directly?

Troubled by his wild assumptions, Skyler scans the metallic chip that Larson fitted on his wristband to unlock the doors. The warehouse is anything but conventional, a dark and dusty corner fallen into disuse with only shadows as its tenants.

"These rich people have it so easy," complains Emily, whose wristband's restricted access must weigh heavily on her. "They can walk around wherever they please, even in some shabby warehouse, no questions asked. No wonder they are involved in illegal activities when Command trusts them so blindly. Justice in all its glory."

"Maybe that's for the best. It's not the kind of place any sane person would want to hang out. I'm sure you're not missing out on anything."

"We'll find out soon enough."

The last beams of light fade, giving way to cold thickening darkness that tears through Skyler's stomach. They came here to save starving illegal babies who might have poisoned themselves with the formula that's supposed to feed them. Nothing to do with dealing illegal drugs, right?

"Just great," grumbles Emily from somewhere in front of him. "This place is dark as a tomb. How can we possibly find the smuggler? I can't even see my own feet! And this horrible rotting smell is going to make me sick!"

The smell is so strong that Skyler feels like he's reliving his first autopsy. He didn't perform it himself, of course, but every medical student is required to attend the procedure, or what they call a rite of passage. It is the first class they must attend at the Academy because death is the very foundation of the Ark, and the thing they will always have to deal with in their profession—the one unwavering constant.

During that class, the faint of heart had either vomited or fainted. Skyler was in the first group. Even the pervasive smell of fish hanging for weeks throughout the ship during the busy harvest season, when shoals of fish are especially abundant, is hardly enough preparation to cope with the foul stench of a decaying body. Not to mention that they use a saw in this first course, rather than a laser to cut through flesh and bones to reveal the internal organs. Another reminder of the despicable circumstances in which humans lived on the Surface. As barbaric as it sounds, it is necessary to determine the cause of death, and prevent the rapid spread of a pathogen among the survivors. Luckily, none of the victims affected by the stigmata will die, or else he already knows where they will be headed next. If he ever gets stuck in the morgue, it will be all thanks to

Larson using his influence against Skyler. That could very well be how this evening concludes if they fail this mission.

"It's not that far from reality," replies Skyler, who can detect the smell of chemical compounds as they bathe in a foul cloud of fermentation.

Emily gasps as a frantic scratching noise follows.

"Are you okay?" he asks. "Careful out there. We could be in a morgue."

"Don't tell me I just brushed a dead man's toe!" squeaks Emily, uncharacteristically.

"I thought your father trained you the Paragon way."

"I was taught to fight, not to play with a corpse, damn it!"

"That's about right," someone says in the darkness. Skyler jerks around. "Careful. The dead don't like wandering hands."

"Mara," says Emily, dumbstruck. "What the hell are you doing here?"

The drug dealer from the Delta greenhouse? No way…

"I followed your scent, honey."

Skyler tenses up, thinking back on the petty smile she wore as she was replenishing her supply of psychoactive seeds.

"Third time's the charm, right? Though I didn't think you would come here to have a blast with your boyfriend. You've got weird taste, honey."

"You have it all wrong," Skyler cuts. "We did not come here to listen to your nonsense."

"You should learn to relax a little, Doc. No offense, but you're doing a lousy job at it."

"Are you done yet?"

"All right, all right. Come right this way."

Emily's hand slips into Skyler's—the texture is unmistakable with the lack of light heightening his senses. This smuggler must be guiding Emily in the same way and be very familiar with this place because she stops abruptly only once to avoid some invisible wall. They walk across another section of the warehouse, wedged deeper in the darkness. Skyler is eager to get a breath of fresh air—at least the closest thing he can get in a dilapidated ship—but his mood darkens rather quickly.

Burning flesh. The smell twists his insides.

"What a place to meet," coughs Skyler while covering his nose.

"Nasty, I know," says Mara, whose features glow in the embers of a flame burning nearby in some kind of well. "Not for long, though. They'll be making their rounds soon."

"Who exactly are we talking about?" asks Emily as she peers at the roaring well.

"The Paragon, of course," replies Mara, who doesn't seem bothered either by the stench or the sweltering heat, hot enough to warp the sheet metal of the walls. "They've got to clean up their mess."

The roaring fire casts its glow over the emaciated shapes of corpses in the passage they just came from. Emily shuts her eyes while rubbing her hand against her clothes. Skyler cannot imagine how these people died and why they are not properly stored in a refrigerated morgue. Their rapid decomposition is inevitable, as is the spread of any communicable disease. Considering the ship's antiquated ventilation system, this is neither desirable nor logical.

Mara slips back into the darkness and tells them to follow her. She giggles when she sees Emily's frightened look.

"This is the right way if you're interested in the miracle powder, and that way if you want to end up in the incinerator."

"I'm not going to flirt with corpses in the dark. I'd like to keep my pure, innocent teenage mind the night before my graduation. Adulting starts tomorrow. No sooner."

"Dead people can't talk or move, Emily," says Skyler, leaving the warmth of the alcove. "That's why they're dead. You're safe as long as you don't try to wake them."

"Aren't you supposed to provide comfort to your terrified patients?"

Skyler follows the smuggler, who doesn't wait for Emily to stop whining. How could a few corpses scare Emily Bates of all people? Wasn't she excited to track down a legendary underwater monster who devours not only its victims' entrails, but their grieving souls in a hellish world?

They walk back into this lightless world made of air fluctuations and putrid smells. Mara doesn't offer him a hand to guide him—not that he minds; the last thing he wants is befriending a drug dealer—but he keeps an ear out for the rustle of her footsteps and the sound of her voice.

"They've done everything they can to erase this place from the ship's records," Mara explains, "because whoever controls it has full power over the Command."

"Control of a morgue?" says Skyler, stumped as Emily's labored breathing comes closer.

Is she seriously terrified? They're just dead bodies.

"You'll see."

After a while, the air smells of a sickening sweet aroma similar to the waffles they sometimes serve at breakfast.

"Jesus does this place lead straight to the dining hall kitchens?" stutters Emily. "Tell me that's not the food they serve, or I'll never eat again."

"They know about the illegal babies," Mara says in a strange voice. "They've always known. They developed a foolproof security system—if you can call it that—that tricks the senses. What would illegals do if they starved enough to risk their lives for a bite?"

What future would await the child if Skyler had not entrusted him to the sanctuary? In a few years, malnutrition would eat away at his gaunt face and frail body. But most of all, the boy would face a hopeless choice: starve and die, or eat the bait and die of food poisoning.

Is this all the empathy and compassion the Ark can show? Have they learned nothing from the Furies, when Skyler's grandparents were still in their youth and overpopulation made passengers kill each other over a piece of rotten fish? Any practice from that dark period in their history should be abolished. And yet, the Paragon resorts to questionable practices shamelessly. What about the Commander?

"Without this special tool, you will set off the alarm," says Mara. She is gently whipping the air with some flexible metal stick that gives off a dim light and bends with her motion. "Lucky for us, I got what we need."

"Why would you choose such a risky place to deal? Right in the lion's den," says Emily with a hint of anger in her voice.

"That's the point. Nobody would expect that."

Mara lights up a section of the wall where a tile shifts under her fingers. They take turns slipping through the open space and enter another warehouse, lit up by the Ark's night light. At this hour, bluish light beams run against the walls. As Skyler's vision adjusts, he spots a row of crates stacked on either side, making it seem like an orderly maze. The smuggler discards her stick near a heavy crate. She cracks it open, revealing bags filled with a grayish powder like the one in Larson's lab, but not quite.

"Larson's stocks are safe," she says, "but we'll need to refill soon. I don't understand why he doesn't come and see for himself, but geniuses are hard to understand sometimes. His message about you was sketchy, though. His brother usually does the dirty work for him."

"Kahlo would never get involved in this business," Emily protests.

"Believe me. He's been at it for a while. Why do you even care? Are you chasing after the White brothers? Good luck with that. They're as tight as a drum. I, on the other hand, am open to offers."

"What's the most effective way to get rid of this powder?"

replies Skyler, who doesn't care in the least how the White brothers spend their free time or what Mara's advances are.

"Are you kidding?"

"We need a sample first," says Skyler. Larson gave them clear instructions before taking off the metal piece clasped on his wristband, which sent him a sharp jolt of electricity. "That's what Larson wants."

The smuggler raises her voice a notch.

"We finally have a way to rescue the Mav—"

"I don't make the rules. Didn't you say the Paragon's next round at the morgue is coming up? I'd like to get this over with once and for all. This evening has gone on long enough."

The built-up tension is putting him on edge, and the more time he spends with this drug dealer, the higher the chances he could do things he will later regret. With that sickening smell to top it all, his patience to bargain is running thin.

"Larson can't just dump our inventory."

Mara is also an illegal. The evidence strikes him all at once. How to convince her?

"This powder is contaminated. If they drink it, they'll die."

He can't skimp on his words, or she'll never agree to do what Larson expects of them.

"You've got no proof, Doc," she defends herself. "As far as I know, you're not a chemist. You bring down fevers and patch up dangly bits of flesh."

"Larson himself suspects there's something wrong with the powder. Would you have a clear conscience knowing that your people could die because of you? Just imagine the bodies."

She has a moment's hesitation, eyebrows furrowed.

"There are too many casualties on this damn ship," she snorts with an impish grin.

"And we have a way to avoid it. So how do we get rid of this powder?"

Since the illegals expect to receive the ration they were promised, Mara tells them that the safest way to make sure none of her people—Skyler was right to believe she was an illegal—stumble upon the supplies is to burn the crates contents in the incinerator. Skyler worries about the toxic fumes that might escape, but they won't be around long enough to feel the effects. If the independent ventilation system can filter out the latent fumes of cremating bodies, a few pounds of food powder shouldn't be too much to handle. That is, if the contaminant does not react to the flames, but Skyler keeps that comment to himself. He wouldn't want Mara to change her mind.

For fear the Paragon will arrive any minute to patrol, they set out to pass around the bags one at a time to the incinerator. The mind-blowing amount of powder Larson has managed to produce on his own is staggering. His project must have a long history.

Each time they pour out the powder, the flames turn shades of purple, green, and blue, just like the aurora borealis found at the Earth's poles, when their planet's geomagnetic shield and the overwhelming solar wind clash violently. In their science class, when Skyler was only twelve, they were shown the only photograph of this heavenly show preserved in the Archives. A mere glimpse of what's up there, but a priceless treasure, nonetheless. Ever since, Skyler had wanted more: to feel the cool wind bite his skin and make his eyes water, to stretch his neck until he feels dizzy and beat the snow with his boots to warm his toes, to spend a little more time taking in Mother Nature's slow dance in front of his children. This would be the way to ask forgiveness for their past mistakes, one that can rekindle their stormy relationship and pave the way to a better future where they need each other.

The life-hungry flames in the pit's hearth baffle him. Is that all he will ever know: death hiding behind these metal walls, waiting for the right time to strike them down? Why can't they just stop feeding this fire that destroys them?

"Shit!" mutters Mara, who returns to the last remaining crates at the other end of the huge warehouse. A strong smell of burning grass wafts over them, along with laughter and footfalls. Three beams of light bounce over the stack of metal crates, the only thing that stands between them and their unwanted guests.

The Paragon has arrived.

Skyler leans his head against a crate, shutting his burning eyes. Why do those agents always keep coming tonight?

Based on their casual tone and laughter, these three do not appear to be on duty. Their exchange makes little sense as well. They are talking about octopuses, and how the guy got his head sucked in as he tried to smack his lips against it. Skyler can't help but glare at Mara.

"Customers of yours?" he hisses.

"Whatever I need to survive," she retorts.

"Isn't the man we saw in Delta labs your father? Doesn't he help you financially?"

"Dez doesn't share his wealth. He'd rather disown his daughters and leave them to rot in the lower levels."

"Why don't you take care of your customers so we can get the hell out of here?" says Skyler, squeezed in at an angle to avoid the beam of light swaying dangerously in his direction.

Without warning, Mara jumps out of their hiding spot, squinting at the lights making her look like a ghost. The agents lower their flashlights when they recognize her.

"Well, if it isn't the merchant of dreams!"

"How about an all-inclusive trip to a psychedelic world?" Mara replies in a tempting voice.

"Sounds like the ark to me," says the first one.

"Can't afford it," says the other. "We need to get up early

tomorrow for the ceremony. If Duke Kay catches us in the hammock of heaven, we're screwed. He'll notice if our ranks are not perfectly aligned."

"Not the hammock, idiot! It's the stairway to heaven."

"What's a stairway again?"

With one hand behind her back, Mara motions for Skyler and Emily to come out of their hiding place and make a run for it. They sneak out under the cover of the bright flashlights, but one of the two guards blocks their way, slumped against a pile of crates, too drunk to stand.

"Too bad," says Mara, trying to stall for time. "Today was the first harvest of Arahmis seeds. I guess I'll have to find someone else to buy my top-quality seeds, then."

Mara pretends to walk back toward the opposite direction, but a woman Skyler had not noticed brandishes an electric prod that ripples through the air in an angry hiss.

"There's no negotiating, merchant of dreams. Those idiots might play along, but not me."

"They have a good reason to, though," Mara replies while stepping back. "If their secret got out, they'd be executed on the spot. These trips on the stairway to happy land have a cost, after all."

The drunken agent shifts, but now his body blocks the way out, trapping Mara. Out of the corner of her eye, she watches Skyler and Emily sneak into the unexplored confines of the warehouse. The female agent notices Mara's expression and follows her gaze.

Skyler and Emily bolt forward in the unknown, as shouts of surprise shoot behind them. Blind, Skyler slams a hand against a wall and runs his fingers along to find a way out. The Paragon's flashlights cast their ominous lights sporadically on different sections of the metallic wall, and when a beam hits the familiar outline of a door, Skyler uses the chip on his wristband to open it. The door unlocks as he expected—being a White on this ship definitely has its perks—and their pursuers freeze.

Skyler quickly launches himself inside, heart pounding, but the ground slips away. The void tugs at him, and while he reaches out to grab onto something to stop his fall, the kiss of death drags him into an enveloping darkness.

9

THE THERMAL SHOCK IS BRUTAL.

With no landmarks to find his bearings, Skyler flaps his arms in a fierce struggle against the water cage that keeps him trapped. Panic overtakes him as there are no lights pointing to the surface. He groans at the strong pressure in his nose, then he feels a trail of bubbles coming out of his mouth. He places his hand near his lips to feel where the bubbles are rising. He shifts in the same direction. As the pressure in his nose decreases, he pushes with his legs to propel himself up to the surface.

He spits out brackish water and gasps for air, all the while trying to silence the panic threatening to take over his body—the fall, the darkness, the abyss, a story repeating itself.

No. He is alive, even if he is clueless about his whereabouts. The cold water stirs around him in a choir of splashes that sings his return to life. But for how long?

Did he fall into one of the Paragon's loading bays? The relic hunter pools are on the opposite side of bay seventy-seven, the only likely place to hold a significant amount of water on board. There could be a breach in the ship's hull, but Command would have warned the Archeans, wouldn't they?

Emily's familiar cry comes right before a splash of water that catches him by surprise. He swallows water and wheezes through a coughing fit as he pictures himself sinking to the bottom of the water, drowning. Luckily, his coughing fades into a lasting echo. The room must be rather large by the sound of it. He focuses, hoping to pinpoint Emily's location.

Silence.

After a minute, Skyler can't wait any longer and swims over to the earlier splash's general direction. What if she is stuck at the bottom? Even if he dove, it would be useless! He hits the water hard to guide Emily as to where the surface is.

There is a gasp further away. She is alive!

This world of darkness clutches his throat while he shouts her name as if his life depends on it. Water finds a way into his mouth again, but this time he spits it out immediately.

"We're screwed," Emily says in a choked voice. "How are we going to get back up in this darkness?"

"You shouldn't have followed me. It's all my fault."

"I jumped in willingly, Sky! Larson White is the problem. We wouldn't be in this mess if he hadn't teamed up with a bunch of drug dealers to supposedly help out starving illegals with his dangerous magic powder."

"Still, it's my fault. I should have made for the warehouse entrance."

Emily sighs loudly.

"Excuses will get us nowhere. The Paragon won't come to our rescue this time, and Mara, well she's too busy winning over that agent through a tangle of lies."

Something raspy rubs against Skyler's leg, and his heart stops.

"Emily, was that you?"

No response. That raspy sensation, again, but sharper this time, as if someone was having fun scratching his leg with long, sharp nails.

Like Edelsa Harris when she saw a hologram—arguably much more realistic than those of the cats—of a land mammal in the Academy biology class not so long ago: a plump, hairy chimpanzee with its pink tongue sticking out, its canines flashing. The terror had spread like a ripple among the students, Edelsa included. The class that was supposed to teach them what their primate ancestors looked like had become a horror movie, with the most traumatic animal in the Ark's history, superseding the feral cat infestation. The situation had taken an unexpected turn: a debate about the origins of life that got out of hand. No one wanted to admit having any connection with that kind of monster. Skyler would never understand why—nature can do wonderful things—but some people doggedly refuse to accept what they don't want to see, no matter what.

Edelsa's fingernails had left red marks on his arm for three days, and his parents had plied him with a bunch of questions about those unusual marks. The Goldbergs wanted anything but to get entangled in misunderstandings with the other powerful families; especially his father, who depends on their favor to give priority to oceanography which usually does not garner much attention among the many departments at the Deltas. Instead of delegating some of their research, the Deltas prefer to keep everything under their control, even if this means neglecting some areas of research they deem less important for the Archeans.

"Skyler! Something's in the water, and it's big. Too big," says Emily, her voice quivering.

Skyler's skin is burning, but he can't figure out how bad it is in the water. He tries to sense a presence, but he can't feel anything in this dark, shuttered space.

"How do you know? We can't see anything in here."

"I can feel it. I don't know how to explain."

Emily has always had these funny hunches and her own ways of noticing details that a normal person would miss. Some kind of sixth sense that others don't have. In med school, they learned that a small percentage of the population, mostly women, have a genetic mutation called tetrachromacy, where a fourth photoreceptor cone dramatically expand their color scheme. Whether Emily has this mutation or not, he cannot tell for sure, but nothing else seems to explain her enhanced night vision.

"Oh my God! Don't move."

Something is approaching, or so he thinks, or rather feels. Darkness shifts about, coiling around him. Is this a product of his imagination? This darkness is driving him crazy!

Time slows down with the huffing and puffing of their breaths, as if conspiring against them. Either they make it out alive, or they don't. That thing grazes at his leg again just as Emily lets out a scream seconds later. How long is this thing? Could there be more than one?

Skyler doesn't want to be its next meal by standing around, so he swims with all his might toward Emily's whimpering. That's when he sees them.

Two bright red eyes staring at him from an impossible height above the water's surface. Emily grabs his hand and leads him away, but he cannot take his eyes off that living thing. They let go of each other's hands, and Skyler dives underwater to swim faster. The pounding of his heart reminds him that he is not hallucinating and still well and alive. This thing could pull him away from Emily at any moment. Maybe it's letting him escape on purpose, just so it can play with them later, enjoying every bit of its hunt. There is probably nothing like the taste of fear flowing in their weak flesh.

When he emerges, the spotlights light up one after another, followed by an ear-splitting screech.

"Get out now!"

Skyler blinks, dazzled by the sudden brightness that floods the room. On a two-story-high platform, Mara motions for them to hurry. Next to her is the female Paragon agent from earlier who is pale with fear.

"Skyler!" Emily shouts.

Shiny scales glint on the sea serpent's head floating soundlessly on the water's surface, the slits of its glowing eyes darting at them. This thing can't be real and yet…

"Is this the Leviathan you were talking about?" he asks Emily, completely dazed.

"I don't… I …," Emily stammers.

Nothing prepared them for this. The Academy showed them all sorts of animals, ranging from the most harmless creatures to a handful of predators, but nothing like this … thing watching them, brushing the surface with its head. Skyler swims sideways, his eyes locked on the snake, as if that could ward off a potential attack.

With cautious haste, Skyler and Emily reach the metal platform that surrounds the gigantic pool where they fell. The snake dives back into the water. Skyler wonders for a moment if what he witnessed was a dream, but then the creature whisks its tail across the surface, and a misty spray rains on them.

"I wouldn't wish that on my worst enemy," says the Paragon agent standing near the exit, pale as a corpse.

"Why didn't it attack us?" asks Emily, wringing out her clothes.

"The light blinds it," explains the agent. "In the dark, it is a fearsome creature, a predator of the ever-changing waters of the Great Ocean. The Flood was a calamity for land creatures, but it's stimulated mutations of the marine fauna to levels never before seen. Food is plentiful and predators are thriving from feeding tenfold. A direct consequence of their new diet is their increased size and mass."

"So, the Leviathan legends are true," says Emily in a strangled voice.

"Isn't there some truth to them to start with?" says Skyler, who can hardly believe what he is saying.

"Why was this creature brought on the Ark?" asks Emily to the Paragon agent, who's glowering at her.

"Why was a teenage girl wandering about the Paragon's warehouse in the middle of the night? Civilians are not allowed here. The Academy should have made that clear a long time ago, or they aren't teaching you anything useful and wasting my time. I could arrest you for this."

"But you won't," Emily retorts defiantly, while putting her soaked hair back in place.

"It was the wrong thing to say," mutters Mara, who had kept silent until then. Her eyes are fixed on the last ripples in the pool, perhaps imagining ways to get her hands on the Leviathan's scales. She could add a fine new mind-altering drug to her inventory.

"Why not do things differently for once?" the agent sneers. Skyler would give anything to face the Leviathan rather than seeing what she could do to them.

"Even if you wanted to, I don't see how you could arrest three people by yourself," Emily adds.

"I have no part in this," Mara replies. "Our deal was scrapped as soon as you tried to get away."

"No wonder, coming from a drug dealer," hisses Emily. "You're all the same. Selfish to the core."

"I kinda liked you, but I'm having second thoughts on helping you out," Mara replies.

Skyler joins Emily and whispers, "We knew what we were getting into when Larson set us up. Given the chance, Mara would have walked out on us, anyway."

Meanwhile, the agent went out into the hallway to seek out her two teammates snoring against the crates.

"*Pendejos*, let's go. With the kids."

The two men growl, the agent slaps them without hesitation.

"I said let's go! And watch them," she barks. Then, with pursed lips, she turns to Skyler and Emily, "Don't even think about running away or the charges against you will be even worse."

"Told you so," Mara says with a snide look for Emily. "Not sure you'll be able to fix this one," she adds for Skyler. "You'll have to find someone to lick your wounds, and fast."

As the magnetic handcuffs snap around their wrists, Skyler feels a trickle of blood running down his leg.

10

"IT'D BETTER BE WORTH IT."

The petite redheaded woman adjusts her suit briskly as she enters the room with a firm step. The office is set up in a huge cabin reserved for important members of the Ark's system, away from the residential sector where the Goldbergs live. Every surface including the walls are in pristine condition, covered with velvet the color of a pale salmon marinating in its oil. The air smells of oil and candlelight that has been burning for too long. The strange intimacy of the cabin orders him to forget this place and turn back at once.

What a weird place to have an interrogation.

Despite his towering height, the man closely following the suited woman moves like a ghost and blends into the background: his transparent skin, unnaturally white hair, and statuesque figure would look good at Adeline White's party.

It must be well past midnight, and the suited woman's stony face speaks volumes about her displeasure. She pulls up her collar, and Skyler catches a glimpse of a hickey, a trend that has been spreading like wildfire at the Academy lately. Edelsa even tried to give one to Skyler. That's when he knew it was time to put some distance between them before he found himself married with children.

Ready to press charges against them, the Paragon agent Emily has deliberately offended stays quiet. Meanwhile, the suited woman's lackey retreats in an adjoining room lodged into the mesmerizing velvet folds resembling human tissue, and simply by looking at it, Skyler feels sucked into an imaginary esophagus about to douse him with acid. When he comes back, the man is holding a coffee cup he hands over to the suited woman, who then takes a slow sip. She breathes a deep sigh.

"These two youngsters are guilty of multiple offenses," begins the agent, standing ramrod straight. "They trespassed in bay seventy-seven, damaged an experimental subject in the Paragon training room..."

That's where they met the aquatic creature that was caught near the Flaminis's ruins for a detailed analysis of the mutations it has undergone since the Flood. Undeterred by their predicament, Emily fired questions at the Paragon agent on their way to the suited woman's cabin. Despite the agent's surly look, she gave away this information while they were waiting, to silence Emily, perhaps?

"This thing almost ate us alive!" shouts Emily, unimpressed by the prominent member of the Command and the colossus who could suck out their souls at any moment.

"Possibly involved in the White case," adds the agent, raising her voice. "My partner, Officer Fish, says he witnessed her colorful performance that stirred up trouble during the evening."

"Where is this Fish, Agent Perez?" asks the suited woman with a hint of annoyance.

"Waiting outside."

"The slacker snoring in my hallway? Who would be stupid enough to do this! How unprofessional!"

"It's been a long night for all of us," stutters the agent.

"And yet here we are at an unearthly hour. At your request. Which brings me to the question, why did you come to me and not Duke Kay? Would he have tolerated such a faux pas?"

"Agent Mirza, I—"

"Warden Mirza. The procedures laid out by the Commander are clear. Unless an unforeseen event prevents the leader of the Paragon from dealing with this matter, under no circumstances should a mere agent such as yourself communicate directly with the warden of the Ark's prison."

The Ark's prison, no more and no less, a one-way ticket into a cell—Skyler tenses up, concerned. Shouldn't they be entitled to a proper trial at the hexagon of Great Justice?

"I remember our last meeting, Warden Yasmina Mirza, but especially your promise." The warden frowns at that.

"I don't promise anything without something in return."

The agent is unswayed and opens the door so abruptly that Skyler thinks she's going to jump out. The so-called Officer Fish wakes up with a start, slumped at the foot of the opposite wall, and stares blankly at them. His nose hair extends into a bushy mustache that hisses every breath he takes.

"Fish, explain exactly what Emily Bates did," orders Agent Perez, who is intent on convicting them.

The agent looks down and gives him the floor. Fish staggers inside under the warden and her unblinking lackey's steely gaze.

"I was on duty with my partner Chips," the mustached man begins hesitatingly, glancing around as if the walls were alive. "We knew the White's party was going to be major, so we loaded up on energy drinks."

"Get to the point," Agent Perez urges him, head down.

"All right. Emily Bates arrived a little later than the other guests, wearing a dress just like my mother wore on the Sunday sanctuary service. She said this ship was drab and a touch of purple might—"

A sigh of frustration coming from the agent unnerves him and he picks himself up, raising his tone, looking nervous and irritated.

"She was accompanied by one of the White brothers, so there was no need to ask any question. If the boys decide to bring over a pretty girl, there's nothing we can do about it."

Fish catches his breath, clearly fighting a bout of dizziness, but so far, he has managed to deftly keep the side effects under control. But for the trained eye, you would think he's just a little clumsy. "The evening was going well, except for the usual snaps between the Yangs and the other guests. Chips and I were feeling hungry, but someone had to stay at the entrance, so I volunteered to get something from the buffet. Emily Bates was also there … bonding with one of the White brothers."

Stunned, Skyler looks at Emily who blushes for the first time ever since he's known her. In fact, her face reddens when she gets angry, but never for any other reason.

"Her bag should have been checked just like any other guest, but Chips forgot. So, I asked to see her bag, but she refused to cooperate. I reminded her that she has no right to resist the Paragon, but she bit back and threatened me."

How can he pretend to be the victim when he has a gun and a prod within reach? It's laughable, even though Emily usually likes to make a point about everything and stir up trouble.

"She protested angrily and accused me of harassing her," he says, looking genuinely troubled. "I've been a loyal agent to the Paragon for years, and this brat wrongfully accuses me of harassment."

"Is that all?" cuts Warden Mirza with an eye roll.

"She took my gun and threatened me! In front of everyone!"

"Don't leave out the part where you almost had me kneel in public," Emily scolds. "I'll never submit to the Paragon's whims, you hear me? I should've used that goddamn electric prod to see what it can really do."

Emily's burst of anger earns her a smile from the warden.

"That's what I thought. She's a threat to our security! *Loca!*" says the female agent with a horrified expression.

"Impressive," purrs the warden, blatantly ignoring the female agent. Her eyes shine with interest in Emily, who is probably holding back a snide remark.

Emily is more controlled than usual today, probably stunned by fatigue. It seems that this is her trial and hers alone; Skyler feels a twinge of sadness. Emily is reckless by nature, true, and her family wasn't as fortunate as the Goldbergs, but it should not be used against her. This is wrong, but how do you change other people's minds?

Officer Fish continues, more alert than ever, his mustache twitching with his breath.

"She attacked me, then ran away from the party, causing quite a ruckus. Chips and I chased her to the gardens, but then, things went south. This other kid got involved, and they locked us up by setting off the security system. We almost froze to death in there!"

"I can't believe it was those two idiots shooting at us," Emily, who slipped by his side while the others were too busy arguing, whispers in Skyler's ear.

"Why didn't you tell me before?" says Agent Perez, who finally raises her head. "I'm the leader of this squad!"

"So you can get in my face? I know what happens if we fail on a mission, Stefania."

"Silence!" cuts in Warden Mirza unflinching, her voice alone having the effect of a bomb. "What about her?"

The warden points a finger at Mara, who has managed to avoid everyone's attention so far, including Skyler's, who forgot she was even there. Mara is rubbing her face against the velvet wall, giggling uncontrollably.

"Mara helped me catch these kids," says the worried Agent Perez. "They were planning to take part in drug trafficking."

Mara blinks at that, yanked out of her drug-induced mind trip that was supposed to keep her safe from reality. Before Skyler can speak up, the warden walks over to Emily with a broad smile showing her prominent cheekbones.

"Of course not. Emily Bates wouldn't do something like that, would she? Given her … questionable past. What a disgrace that would be!"

Despite Emily's quick temper, Skyler can't stand to see her being morally harassed in this way.

"Before accusing us of drug trafficking, you should take a closer look at those Delta greenhouses."

"And you are?"

"Skyler Goldberg," he says, swallowing hard.

How does Emily put up with being the center of attention? He would give anything not to have all those eyes tracked on him. Emily has come to his rescue countless times, so he owes her at least that much.

"Ah… Goldberg," says the warden. "Your father is an oceanographer if I remember correctly? He works a few meters away from the greenhouses—a witness, in that case. Tell me more."

"For a guided tour, I suggest asking her," he replies by pointing at Mara who freezes instantly.

The warden lets out a peal of laughter. The trafficker clearly does not realize the consequences of her illicit activities, let alone the ripple effect it has on everyone aboard. She must be stopped while there is still time.

The warden lowers her shaking finger slowly. Then, she brings her hands together, her posture straight as a metal wall of the ship.

"Agent Perez, Stefania Perez, I should say. After all, we've known each other for some time. I appreciate your dedication, but between you and me, your squad is sorely lacking. Let me be frank with you: your agents are a bunch of incompetents.

How could Fish and Chips—what stupid names, by the way— fail to stop the young Bates from escaping Adeline White's private party, when the guests' safety was their responsibility? Not to mention leaving an unchecked bag, which could have concealed a lethal weapon, unattended."

The suited woman smirks at these words.

"We can never be too careful ever since the Furies. Our God-sent commander moves heaven and earth to keep us alive as long as possible, but if our home is teeming with weeds, some-thing must be done swiftly with regard to the procedures put into place. Otherwise, this ship isn't going anywhere."

"But still, I—"

"You violated the Paragon's protocol by disturbing me at an ungodly hour! Has it not occurred to you that the guardians of this ship need to rest as well?"

Warden Mirza scratches the mark on her neck as the female officer swallows hard, disbelieving.

"Such fools," she hisses with disgust.

"You said you were … looking for leads on the stowaways," says Agent Perez, who mysteriously recovered her voice. "I did."

"Those fabled nameless illegals."

The warden's eyes shine with obvious interest at the mention of these poor children. The face of the little one Skyler entrusted to Mrs. Farrell flashes in his mind, asleep and unaware of the danger lurking; a danger fueled by the greed and lack of empathy of a handful of Archeans acting in the name of their so-called justice. Skyler hopes the warden is not one of them.

"Getting information about them is crucial to meet the Commander's expectations," she adds, biting her lips. "What did you find?"

"You can ask Emily Bates about it," says Agent Perez, with sweat beads shining on her eyebrows.

The warden glances questioningly at Emily, who is silently

brooding, Skyler can tell by the way she is mindlessly wringing her hands. The Emily he knows would pounce on the agent for falsely accusing her if she were not handcuffed. All things considered, Emily would still give it a try. Her father trained her to defend herself with every part of her body. What is she up to?

"What about our deal?" Agent Perez says impatiently, avoiding Emily's gaze.

"I'll see if the results are satisfactory enough," replies the warden, staring back at her.

"I have nothing to do with these illegals, but she does," says Emily, pointing with her chin at Mara, still quiet and obsessed with the velvet.

Deep in her thoughts, the warden doesn't respond right away and goes back to her desk while keeping her head down. Skyler recognizes the familiar lullaby she is humming. He heard it during a visit in the birthing department at Med Bay, right before the nurse would step into compartment zero with a baby.

"Ludovic."

The ghostly man comes to life at the sound of his name, freed from his marble prison. Agent Perez seems to understand what is happening. She steps forward and quickly spouts, "Mara was instrumental in capturing these two—"

"I'm aware of that, as well as your squad's questionable ties with the enemy," the warden replies, as if lecturing a child caught red-handed. "For professional reasons, of course, but trying to cover up one's misdeeds in the Paragon's eyes, and therefore our justice system, is unacceptable. The Theta Division cannot afford to let a free spirit roam the ship and suggest that we show leniency to those who betray us. You can't stand on the fence, Agent Perez. We are either with or against the Commander. He would hate to think that such … people are plaguing the ranks of his armed forces. The immunity that comes with the Paragon is too important for me to turn a blind eye on this unacceptable behavior. I have always stood against this immunity, but the Commander knows best when it comes to protecting us from unfortunate events, but especially from unwanted people."

Ludovic grabs Mara not so gently, despite her cries of protest and her desperate attempt to cling to the velvet wall with her fingernails. She tries to bite him, hissing, but gives up abruptly, her head lolling. A drop of blood beads on her neck which means she was injected with a tranquilizer.

"Agent Perez, would you please leave us alone? I'll inform the Paragon leader of your … find. I'd brace myself if I were you."

Crestfallen, the female agent bolts out, followed shortly by Fish. The warden's stony expression shifts into a meek smile.

Ludovic is holding Mara, so she doesn't collapse, and watches them intently. Warden Mirza paces in front of them, clicking her heels with each stride, thoughtful. Skyler holds his breath, and so does Emily, her anger evaporated. She stares blankly, just like the time her father scolded her for leaving her little sister Gabrielle alone.

Emily never steps down, even in the face of authority. How can the warden tame her so easily?

Warden Mirza paces behind them like a ticking clock, then stops. She brushes her surprisingly rough fingers over Skyler's wrists to uncuff him. The magnetic handcuffs drop and clink on the floor. She does not pick them up.

"No wonder the Goldbergs have earned their good reputation," she breathes softly near his ear. She sneers at his obvious discomfort. "Don't worry. I'm not like Agent Perez."

She gives him a ghost of a smile then politely shows the door. Skyler walks out exchanging a worried look with Emily who mouths,

See you at the labs.

11

Skyler retraces his steps to Delta Labs for the umpteenth time tonight, hoping it will be the last. The spiral of events he and Emily have been dragged into is overwhelming. They have risked everything: their future, their freedom, their credibility. Years of living up to the Ark and their families' expectations do not make them immune to the ironclad law that rules the ship. If Emily were to fall into the Paragon's hands, not even her father, who is an officer himself, could save her from their scrutiny.

There are other punishments other than rotting in a prison cell. Not having a mentor is another way to lead a pitiful life doing odd jobs no one wants like sorting trash or filling up vending machines in the dining hall. Being a shadow of yourself breaks even the most stubborn minds.

It could be even worse. The right of a family and its descendants to have two children could be reduced to one child. If that new generation fails again, they are no longer allowed to reproduce, and the lineage is erased. The Ark would put the blame on a serious genetic problem that could endanger humanity's chances to settle on the Surface. Only honest and honorable families should lay the foundation of civilization 2.0.

Sometimes those who leave a significant mark are granted a third child, but these occurrences are rare. The Academy instructors might be planting seeds in their students' minds just so they behave properly.

Warden Mirza letting him leave her cabin is exceptional. Hopefully, Emily will have the same chance. The last thing he wants is someone from Command wiping out her lineage before she can redeem the Bateses. Emily is strong-willed and resilient like few others: a diamond in the rough waiting to be polished with the right tool to shine through the darkness that has settled over this ship.

The lights in Larson White's lab are still on in the sleepy hallway, a gentle reminder that Skyler should be sleeping right now. With graduation lasting most of the day tomorrow, he can't disappoint his family. That would be one too many times.

The commotion in the lab freezes him mid-stride before crossing the threshold: a sea of broken glass and syrupy liquid with queer smells shower the floor.

"Is this how you use my lab?" shouts Adeline White to her son Larson, who looks troubled, but still in control.

Adeline White is standing near the vines that have taken over the wall where Skyler was trying to identify some exotic species not found in the gardens. The ship's self-proclaimed empress of art nouveau doesn't seem particularly curious or impressed, as she tries to tear off a section of the trellis in a fit of rage. The vine doesn't give, oblivious to the rustling of her dress and the clicking of her heels.

"You grow weeds now?" she adds, shouting. "How do I even know they're not drugs? The White empire was built on the sweat of our family's brow. I won't let you ruin our legacy."

"Whether you like it or not, I am not Kahlo."

From the safety of the passageway's darkness, Skyler recalls the same kind of feuds that break the most tight-knit families. The Goldberg family is no exception. This toxic moment between the Whites will leave an always-festering scar between them.

He wants to leave. The evening has drained him, and the call of his bed is more tempting than ever. But the tracking chip Larson embedded in his wristband for their mission in bay seventy-seven holds him back. The only way is to finish off what they started. Skyler wants to avoid at any cost explaining the situation to his father and have the Deltas remove the chip tampering with his wristband. Since he cannot access his cabin and common areas like the dining hall, he is under Larson's control until he can fix this problem once and for all.

"Are you implying that your upstanding brother is a drug addict? How dare you!"

"Mother, you disappoint me. Have you never suspected his fine looks might cover up some nightly dealings?"

"Don't mix things up. You've been given everything in this life: dreams that no living human being could imagine. You hide an illegal baby in my house pretending to help a classmate who can't babysit her little brother. You kept her name from me, of course, because you know very well that I personally know every single family that lives on this Ark. And you think I can turn a blind eye to your blatant transgressions of the Paragon rules?"

"Maybe you'd see the truth hiding in plain sight if you weren't so busy ogling underwater debris and courting sycophants with wandering hands and easy smiles just to curry their favor. These babies have a right to live. Simply because they were abandoned by their parents does not justify killing them. I guess it's a blessing in a way, since they don't have to deal with obsessive parents who care more about the opinions of others than their own children."

Arms crossed, Adeline White does not recoil from Larson's

imposing stature, which casts a shadow of indifference mixed with deep annoyance at his mother's meddling with his genius.

"Here I thought your taciturn, phlegmatic demeanor hid a rare intelligence," she resumes wistfully, while twirling a potted red flower Skyler missed the first time.

She watches it dance, willing the flower to reveal its hidden beauty, its heart bleeding for all to see. The gravity's pull meets the velvety shield of its petals warding it against the plight of the outside world.

Adeline peels off one petal after another to discover pistils still germinating. Too soon, the flower seems to be saying, as it tries to retract its petals, resisting the assault as best it can. But Adeline White is not the kind of person who waits for things to be ready or beautiful, she pushes them to their limits and forces them to put on a cloak of beauty made of impatience and sweet lies for greedy eyes with misplaced curiosity.

"Great minds can be demanding and unpredictable, even bizarre. Just think of good old Harris with his perfumery of the senses. Make no mistake, he is a dear friend to me, despite his eccentricities. That's why I agreed to give you space, so you can be the next Harris or even Torres, who knows?"

Her voice chokes, and her face takes on a dark hue. She looks around the lab in disgust and bewilderment, the contrast of her fine clothes against the creeping scrub, an unfinished paradox.

"I was wrong."

Her words sound like a death sentence and leave Skyler speechless. Larson, however, stands tall as if wearing an armor of invisible beauty; he is impenetrable.

"I owe it to you for what I've become, Mother," he says with a faint smile. "The cost in human lives your obsession has is staggering. Someone has to clean up after you."

"By defying authority. If your father were still alive, he would set you straight, Larson White. You accuse your own mother of a crime she never committed because you can't accept that the world isn't as pure as you want it to be."

Larson turns on a portable hologram that projects an image of the child Skyler rescued. The baby looks starved and sicker than when he saw him.

"What evil could this child have? Take a good look at him!"

The child is sleeping peacefully in Kahlo's arms in the same lab, but Adeline's gaze does not linger.

"Deal with the Paragon yourself, if that's your wish!" she cries out, throwing her arms in the air.

"You gave me the power to make a difference, and that is what I intend to do."

Larson grabs his mother's arm, and something very strange happens. His pupils dilate unnaturally like a patient under strong narcotics. Adeline White gasps, trying to break free from her son's iron grip. When Skyler decides to step in, Larson lets her drop to the ground as if he had been burned.

Skyler crouches down to examine her, his fears of a potential bacterial contamination the least of his worries. He doubts it has anything to do with what he has just witnessed.

"Why do you care about her?" croaks Larson.

"How can you be so indifferent to your own mother?"

Larson's eyes well up, but he keeps a hard face, "Because I know. I've seen what she really thinks of me."

A hallucination? A powerful psychotic could do something like that. Those notorious Arahmis seeds Mara is dealing on the ship might be involved. What if they are growing in the tangle of roots and plants of this lab?

Skyler checks Adeline White's vital signs and speaks softly to get a response. She looks like she took a powerful blow to her head that knocked her out. This could have happened during her fall, but Skyler glances worriedly at Larson, who rambles on as he inspects the lab thoroughly. All Skyler can hope for is to get Adeline White to Med Bay, that is, if he can convince Larson to let them through.

"I need to get your mother to Med Bay right now."

"Why do you care? Adeline White has caused so much suffering by creating this circle of aristocrats she would call hedonists to ease her conscience. They shamelessly ostracize the Archeans."

Anger blooms in Skyler's throat. How can Larson have such contempt for his own mother? She was thoughtful enough to try to talk him out of his devious plans. If she hadn't cared about him, Larson would be drowning in his own stupidity with no one to stop him.

"Few people are lucky enough to have a mother who cares about their well-being," grunts Skyler, painfully.

"These words are too flattering for Adeline White. She only needed a son shaped to reflect her own image. My little brother Kahlo never complained; he didn't have to. He was our mother's most ardent wish. How many of the Creator's servants did she bribe to make her wish come true? That I'll never know."

"Are you angry at your brother?"

"I love my brother and pity him. I managed to escape our controlling mother's grasp by exiling myself to this lab until she decided to poke around. I tried everything to prove her wrong with the abandoned child I found. Showing her what a pure human life is worth and breaking her sordid ideas molded into the Ark's hull. What wishful thinking! She would have sacrificed him given the chance. What mother worth her salt would do this? Sometimes I envy those abandoned children who don't have to put up with the White's absurd notion. As a Goldberg, you should know." Skyler grinds his teeth. Larson is heading onto a slippery slope.

"What about the illegals? Was that all a lie? You never actually cared about them."

"You're missing the point! I did everything I could to give

them a second chance. They were doomed the moment they drew in their first breath on this cursed ship, with a bunch of servants at the helm, fed by my mother's every whim."

"You say you want to save human lives, but it's just a bunch of nonsense. If you were honest, you would take care of your mother instead of treating her like a piece of trash. Take the damn chip out of my wristband and let me take her to Med Bay."

Fists clenched, Skyler stands up, unsure whether to sabotage the lab or report Larson to the Paragon. He does neither. Justice on this ship has its own rules, and he is not about to throw himself in a game he doesn't quite understand.

Larson sighs angrily, "Fine! But you'll drag her along by yourself."

He grabs a tool lying on the counter where the red flower is losing its luster, the microbial world in full bloom on its petals turning black at a mind-boggling rate.

With a flick of the wrist, the chip finds its way into a trash can, and Larson removes the surgical gloves he had donned specifically for the procedure.

"It's done! Go now before I change my mind."

Larson is busy scrutinizing an invisible experiment going on in his head to escape the dreary reality of what has truly happened in his lab. Skyler should be rushing to Med Bay with Adeline White, but he shakes with rage at Larson's carelessness.

"One day you'll regret this," Skyler says, shakily. "When you've lost her and nothing you can do can save her."

Larson offhandedly ignores him. Skyler bends down to lift one of the most influential women on the Ark, who lies unconscious. He struggles to carry her on his back, his muscles sore by the endless night. He must resort to dragging her along the floor, lifting her by the armpits, until he finds a rolling table in an empty lab that will serve as a makeshift stretcher. The one in the White's lab would do, but Larson might change his mind about showing mercy to his mother.

Down the hall, near a lab with the door left ajar, Larson's voice echoes.

"The experiment can finally begin."

12

Carrying Adeline White to Med Bay turned out to be a harrowing experience. People recognized the Duchess of the Ark—as some call her—lying unconscious. Questions fired up as Skyler made his way through the group of onlookers gathered around the makeshift stretcher. Despite the mysterious bacteria possibly spreading on the ship since the first stigmata appeared, they touched her body mumbling prayers to the Creator, begging for mercy to the woman who worships the cleansing power of their ancestors' works of art. No wonder she is tied to the Sigma Foundation and the Archives of Humanity. People idolize her.

Should she pass away today, not only would they lose an inspiring and ambitious woman, but they would also lose their lens of truth on their stormy past with the Creator. Ignorance is a dangerous window on the world.

After his rescue mission, Skyler fell asleep on a hard bench in the hallway leading up to the operating room, where families hope their loved ones can live another day. The place being empty, he couldn't resist dozing off.

He wakes up in the wee hours of the morning, completely exhausted. Tonight's graduation ceremony looks promising.

Out of curiosity, he asks the receptionist he has run into a few times during his med classes where the Whites are being examined. The room is near the reception desk, plunged into the artificial darkness. Adeline and Kahlo White are lying on two separate beds side by side, with the steady beeping of their heart monitors in the background. He has no idea if they will make it through unscathed. Had he acted sooner, or at least given them proper care on the way, they would have stood a better chance.

How do Dr. Nazar and the others treat people with a mysterious disease? Or handle emergencies properly? With practice and the Creator's will, perhaps, but he will not settle for this easy answer. They cannot constantly rely on the Creator, or they will die before they can go back to the Surface.

"Skyler," Kahlo mumbles, tossing in bed. "You came."

"You should get some sleep," Skyler replies from the doorway. "In a few hours it will be the graduation ceremony."

"I haven't been able to sleep since I found out my mother was admitted. What happened?"

"How should I know?" says Skyler, who doesn't want to get involved in a family quarrel that could turn against him. He learned it the hard way with the Goldbergs.

"I heard you were the one who brought her in," Kahlo adds, sitting up using his elbows. His hands are wrapped in thick bandages. "You saved her."

"I did what I had to do."

"Tell me. Please."

Reluctantly, Skyler recounts the conversation he overheard between Larson and their mother in the lab. Kahlo says nothing, not even about his brother's searing words about their mother and her plans.

"My brother's good," says Kahlo after making sure his

mother is still unconscious. "He's always been. He's told me a few times about his frustration over Mother's plans since our father died, but never directly to her, of course. I can understand why he wants to do things his own way. I might try myself too, if I could, but I don't have his strong will. He's right about one thing: I do like to be told what to do, and frankly I don't mind. Not everyone could bear it, but knowing that it pleases Mother, I will continue to do so."

Skyler had liked the first impression Larson had left him at the party, but in fact, he prefers Kahlo's principled stand much more.

"I didn't come here to put you or Larson on trial, but… I just hope he doesn't do anything stupid. Family comes first."

"Family comes first."

A controversial phrase instilled from an early age. Skyler believed that when people talked about family, they meant all the Archeans, mankind's last great family. His optimism had thrown him in an awkward situation amid a spiritual gathering at the Academy. The Believers had come to his rescue, or rather, seized the opportunity to push the Creator's teachings by using his naive metaphor for themselves. Maybe they were right, but could they see beyond their parents' bedtime stories? He had lost face among the only people he would ever know his entire life. It was a heavy price to pay, but he had learned his lesson; better keep his ideas to himself, and nurture them until the right time comes.

"My brother has his reasons for being mad at Mother and me, but his heart is good." Kahlo winces as he sits in bed. He had forgotten he will not be able to use his hands for a while.

"What did the doctor say?" asks Skyler.

"A severe allergic reaction like he has never seen before."

"That doesn't explain the bleeding."

Only patients who have come into direct contact with acid would have similar lesions, and yet Kahlo's appeared too suddenly. Skyler and Emily could not see anything wrong with him. Kahlo was only holding the child against him, and the fabric was unstained. If the lesions appeared gradually, like an uncontrollable chain break in the capillaries, that would be a different story.

The only way Skyler could find out more would be to examine the wounds himself and run a battery of tests on Kahlo, but he is not authorized to treat patients. For now.

"Do you remember touching anything unusual?"

"I spent the day helping mother set up the art show. You know how important these events are to her and the impact they have throughout the ship. People need them."

The artifacts collected from the sea floor could be contaminated. It is the only valid explanation. Skyler makes a note of it to discuss later with the doctor in charge. It will be the perfect opportunity to stand out for his mentorship, while putting a stop to the spread. If his hypothesis holds true, everyone who attended Adeline White's party is at risk of having come into contact with the toxin. So is everyone who was involved in transporting the artifacts.

However, Adeline White was not affected by the stigmata. She lapsed into unconsciousness with no apparent injury. She obviously spent the most time at the event, probably even helped laying out the display. Her case does not appear to be directly related, though. Could there be something toxic in Larson's lab? Or could Larson himself have poisoned his mother in his fit of anger? The possibility repulses Skyler, who hopes he is wrong. How could a son go to such lengths to get revenge on his mother?

"Isn't Emily with you? She's not hurt, is she?"

"She's being held up," answers Skyler, wondering what happened to her.

She told him she would meet him at the lab, but things may not have turned out in her favor. Did she fall asleep somewhere?

It wouldn't be the first time. If he doesn't see her at the ceremony, he will know something bad has happened. That the warden kept her for further questioning … or worse.

Emily can't miss graduation. She has been talking about it for months.

"Nothing serious, I hope?" asks Kahlo with a worried look.

"You know Emily. She'll find her way out."

"True. I just don't want my dance partner to be missing."

"You asked her to dance during the ceremony?"

Kahlo is shy. How did he muster the courage to ask out the most standoffish girl on this ship? What would his mother say if she knew?

"She did. Should I have turned her down?" Skyler is stunned. Emily usually goes it alone or comes to Skyler when she needs company. But Kahlo White?

"You'll need to rest if you want to make it to the party."

Kahlo nods. Skyler takes one last look at the adjacent bed before exiting, his head buzzing with ideas about the possible ramifications of those stigmata and the dangerous toxin spreading on the ship.

The skin on his hands looks normal. No itching or patches. In short, nothing unusual. Skyler doesn't rule out any possibilities, though. Dr. Nazar's preliminary explanation to Kahlo may only be a way to reassure him. A true diagnosis will take days, even weeks. There are too many unknown variables at this time.

On the way back to his cabin, Skyler imagines what the graduation ceremony will be like, and must face the facts: he won't be able to get away from Edelsa Harris any longer. Emily was supposed to keep him company, but she will be busy with Kahlo White. He is happy for her, but he also feels a twinge of sadness. This will be the first time they won't be together for such an important event. At least, he will be able to find her at the buffet.

If the warden lets her out, of course.

As he nears the Goldbergs's cabin, Skyler slows down, heart pounding in his chest. Someone is waiting by the door, arms crossed.

"Took you long enough."

13

LARSON WHITE STRIDES INTO THE MUTED LAB STILL DRESSED IN his formal wear from the night before, a taste of the oncoming graduation ceremony. In less than a few hours, Skyler will be wearing the outfit Dylan, his father, expressly gave him for the occasion: a navy-blue embroidered uniform with the Goldbergs's signature gold threads. Each family will boast its colors as a reminder of their achievements that tinge the Ark's history, well documented in the Archives of Humanity under the Sigma Foundation's full protection.

Whether Skyler can attend the ceremony depends on Larson, who has dragged him back to the lab. Adeline's eldest son needs his help, and there is nothing Skyler can say to change his mind. As silence sets between them, Skyler can only hope to end their strange cooperation as quickly as possible by giving him what he wants. His father Dylan could get Skyler out of this mess, but the trouble he would have to go through is simply not worth it.

His father would lecture him about shirking his responsibilities and blame Emily for having a bad influence. Skyler will do anything to avoid unnecessary problems with his family.

Larson hangs his jacket on the back of a chair, then rolls up the sleeves of his unbuttoned shirt, revealing marks that tell a different story from what the Whites would have people believe about their family. Bruises of every color mottle his chalky arms. Skyler tenses at what could explain his maiming.

The door shuts with a distinctive click. The last time Skyler heard a clicking sound, he got stuck in their cabin bathroom until his father came back home from work very late that night. Skyler was starving and swore to never lock behind again unless necessary.

He will not be going anywhere anytime soon.

"I don't want to take any chance, since you don't like my tracker," Larson says while tapping his wristband.

The lab has been turned upside down since his last visit. Heaps of uprooted plants are strewn across the countertop, and a new set of vials is distilling some cloudy liquid similar to egg whites. An open package of individually wrapped syringes lying beside confirms Skyler's suspicions: Larson White injects a substance into his veins, and Mara the drug dealer must be working alongside him. This is not a problem Skyler can fix this morning.

Larson is disheveled, the platinum-white hair gleaming under the neon lights, as he rummages through his junk. He didn't mind blackmailing Skyler and sending him down the ship's belly to work with a smuggler last night. What nonsense is he going to ask of him this time? Skyler wishes he could ignore Larson, but his power on the Ark is too great, and his unpredictability could have repercussions beyond the Sigma Foundation. What if Larson could influence the mentorship? If that is the case, Skyler can kiss his chances of becoming a surgeon goodbye.

"You're not very talkative," Larson notes, busy working out the measurements of some liquid solution. "I thought you were more curious by nature. After your successful mission with my contact, I could've pretended our deal never happened. How is my climbing ivy more interesting than I am?"

In her fall, Adeline White tore off part of the ivy hiding a room with fogged windows. When Skyler brushes it with his fingertips while pretending to examine the plant a little closer, a rush of heat tingles his skin.

"It's been a long night," Skyler says in a drawl.

"Sleep is one of the worst plagues of this world. What a waste of time! We need to get rid of this problem in the future."

Judging by the bags under his bloodshot eyes, Larson has not slept for days. He pours the solution into a bottle with jerky movements, not in the least concerned about spilling his precious concoction.

Skyler focuses his attention to the side of the lab that could pass for a small garden. Larson doesn't strike him as a flower enthusiast.

"What is this ivy for? And those flowers over there? I don't remember seeing any in the gardens." White petals with golden-sun hearts crown potted flowers near the heat source.

"The white ones are commonly called chamomile, and the red flowers in the container are cloves picked from the Deltas' clove trees. Ivy is an ideal medicine to treat inflammation. Don't they teach you that in your medical classes?"

"Impressive," Skyler simply replies, recognizing most of the plants in the room.

But that doesn't explain what they're doing in Larson's hands, or how he got them.

Do the Deltas keep private collections of these species in their greenhouses? Shouldn't they be accessible to the public if they have medicinal properties? This doesn't explain why Larson needs these plants, or how he developed a food supplement supposed to feed the ship's illegal babies. Nothing in this lab indicates any protein source whether natural or synthetic. The texture of this egg-white-like liquid maybe, but how does he turn it into a powder? Some crucial elements are missing to explain what is going on here.

"I had to get rid of the nutritional powder because of the mixture," Larson explains to one of Skyler's many silent questions. "The dosage wasn't right."

Skyler frowns as he shifts his attention back to the vial Larson is corking, filled with the same powder they burned in the incinerator.

"How do you know that? Did you test it on them?"

"I'm not that kind of person," Larson snorts, scanning the container at eye level. "I tested it on myself and recorded my observations. I almost died that day. But with this new dosage, they'll have the strength to resist anyone. People like my mother will bend before them."

What kind of experiments does he conduct exactly?

"You can't drug people without their knowledge just because you decide to," says Skyler, quickly identifying the ingredients on the countertop.

A disk of crushed lumps puzzles him. Could it be those Arahmis seeds or something else? Hard to say without tasting it and poisoning himself. The mixture looks fishy.

"Drugs or any form of medication must be tested first. People must consent to the risks involved."

"I know what's good for them. For us," Larson says, weighing his words. Then he puts down the syringe filled with the egg-like liquid and walks over to Skyler, "Isn't that what you want too? That these children may live freely? For the good people, the good humans, to prevail and repopulate the Surface?"

"There must be another way." How can he stop this madness without antagonizing one of the most influential families on the ship?

"It's the only way," Larson replies with ironclad certainty. "People like my mother are bent on having complete control of this ship. Unless someone steps in, it'll be too late."

"You can't really want them dead," says Skyler, who sees no alternative to ending a century-old reign.

Commanders have honored the caste system of the Ark families with their silence, letting the forces at play decide the winners and losers in this micro-society who would eventually establish a colony on the Surface.

The Founders' idea is simple: a ticket in return for working unconditionally for the greater good of mankind. Some have manipulated this promise for profit, for the meaning of the greater good is relative. In the end, there is always a loser.

The Whites are not exempt of this continuing tradition. Adeline White's Sigma Foundation reveals fragments of their past, but at an inordinate cost: exclusivity for those dominating the system. No one objects because they would lose the White's favor if they would.

"Of course not. Their ruling cannot be challenged," Larson grimaces. "But there's a much better way: giving power back in the hands of those who truly deserve it."

Being the White's heir, Larson wants to restore the balance of power with his shady experiments. The Command does not really run this Ark, nor the Paragon that flaunts its colors by wielding their fearsome electric prod, but people like Larson White whose out-of-touch ambitions meet no resistance.

"How?" asks Skyler, genuinely curious. A smile slides across Larson's lips.

"First, you must help with my latest experiment. Nothing too complicated, but very important nonetheless."

He places a rickety metal chair in the only open space of the lab by the fogged-up room, and feverishly rummages through his vials, then chooses three he sets on the countertop beside Skyler. Finally, he grabs two syringes each filled with a different solution and takes a seat on the groaning chair.

"My research is too important to simply disappear if I can't survive. Since our partnership is going well, I figured I could trust you. My options are limited."

"You could have asked your brother Kahlo or Edelsa. We hardly know each other."

"Edelsa had a part to play in my findings, but she won't help me. Actually, she gave me the idea to seek you out. A doctor is exactly what I need to increase my chances of survival."

Skyler peels away from Larson's grinning face to peer into the vials and syringes as he inhales deeply. His hand resting on the counter, he tries to make sense of the mess he's in. No matter how this experiment turns out, Skyler won't be able to walk away unscathed. Who will believe him when his age, experience, and status are all working against him? They will say he is deranged, driven by incoherent fantasies of impressing the Whites while seeking their protection. If an accident occurs, Larson White will never be found guilty of anything. Without the medical knowledge to carry out such experiments, the only culprit will be Skyler who will have helped him. Sacrificing years of his life, his childhood, to work at Med Bay and ruining it all in one night. Skyler scans the locked door but knows very well he is trapped.

Did Edelsa Harris' hold a grudge against Skyler for refusing to marry like their families demand? By using Larson to trap him, she will no longer have to justify why the Goldbergs's son rejected the Harris's heiress. An accidental death can solve this problem easily.

Larson could also be bluffing to cover up his true motive for going after the Goldbergs. Skyler is unaware of what his family might have done to the Whites, but he doubts his parents would chance losing the protection they've enjoyed since Tamara Goldberg's tour de force as the family's true savior. Unless his brother Allen…

"Tell me what to do," Skyler replies, as he keeps staring at the two syringes' mysterious contents.

"Nothing too complicated for a doctor, I assure you. Each bottle contains herbal extracts and medicines to counter specific side effects: inflammation, burns and severe allergies. Just read the label."

Larson explains he will inject his new perfectly dosed concoction himself. Skyler will stay close to assist, should things go awry. At least, Larson does not insist on Skyler giving the injection, nor does he press him with more specific questions. Even though Larson assures him any mishap is unlikely—he's clearly not a doctor to think that way—he would rather not take any chances. He says he had a bad experience once, but does not provide any details, which tickles Skyler. What is he not telling?

"And what is this one for?" asks Skyler, pointing to the remaining syringe.

"You won't need it. It's a gift from Mara. Do you remember her? When her clients have … jolts with the Arahmis seeds, she injects them with this medicine. I accepted just so she would leave me alone. I'd rather stay away from those seeds."

"Haven't you included them in your solution?"

"No. The mixture is unique. If I wanted to experience all the hallucinations my mind is capable of, I wouldn't go to all that trouble. Mara already has everything I need."

Skyler watches Larson roll up his sleeve even further. The way he deftly handles the syringe is painful to watch. Unflinching, Larson injects the liquid pouring it into his veins, and lets the syringe drop on the floor.

"I'm not sure how long it'll take to work," he says, squirming in his chair.

"Thirty minutes for the most severe effects," answers Skyler, recalling his vaccination class. "Up to several days for any latent effect."

"Good. That should do it. I have a doctor with me, anyway."

Despite Larson's confident, almost haughty air, Skyler can see his growing anxiety. He should have asked Larson how to get out of this lab in case they need to go to Med Bay for treatment. Skyler may not have the power to talk him out of going down this slope, but he will not watch him die. Death is a thief Skyler vowed to stop at any cost ever since their fateful encounter.

And yet, its shadow lurks in every corner of the lab, ready to crush them. Not just in this lab, but everywhere on this ship.

"Shit!" screams Larson, his eyes bulging and the nerves in his neck swelling, as if electricity had jolted through him.

Just his luck! Skyler fumbles over the three vials, unsure which to use.

"The code! Give me the damn door code!" shouts Skyler. Med Bay is Larson's only chance for survival. Only the Creator knows what kind of substance is flowing through his veins and attacking his system.

Larson squirms with terrifying grunts. His heavy breathing sounds like his body could give out any moment. The chair's legs slam against the metal in a steady rhythm heralding the reaper's coming.

Skyler knocks down the three vials, smashing a bunch of bubbling containers on the floor at the same time. Fortunately, he palmed the vial for severe allergies, the most likely effective antidote for Larson's violent reaction. He grabs the discarded syringe—never mind looking for a new one—and fills it with the vial's contents. Then Skyler sticks the syringe into Larson's arm and waits for the drug to kick in.

Larson gags, foam gushing out of his mouth, and yanks Skyler's hand. A sudden blinding light bursts between them.

In the darkness of the Goldbergs's cabin, his mother Murielle is holding a candle, her eyes red from too much crying, staring right back at him. The flickering flame paints dancing shadows on her face.

Breathless, Skyler breaks contact with Larson who slumps to the floor, knocking the chair over with a crash. He is unconscious. Skyler kneels to check his vitals. There is no pulse, neither in the wrist, nor in the neck.

Woozy, Skyler staggers back a step, then runs over to the lab door to wrench it open. He wants out, now! His mother's face is still etched in the back of his mind, and he presses his palms against his eyeballs to erase what he just saw. Heaving and confused, he turns on the lab sink's tap and splashes icy water on his face. His hands numbed by the cold, he stops the gushing water, his whole body shaking. Face still dripping, he scans the lab for a solution, but his vision blurs.

What the hell was that?

Larson is slumped all over, his platinum-white hair slowly soaking up the cocktail of liquids that have spilled out of the beakers. Without Larson's access, Skyler must find another way out, and fast, before it's too late. No one will come check this place out except for Adeline or Kahlo who are both bedridden.

The last syringe containing Mara's medicine is still intact despite the sorry mess. Panicked, Skyler quickly grabs it, then injects it onto Larson's lap. He hates himself for using a substance he knows nothing about. What if he just finished Larson off?

Holding his head, he can feel the hell he thought he had escaped coming back at him in a rush. What is wrong with him? Before Larson touched him, he was doing just fine! He was sane!

Coughing. Skyler looks up in disbelief.

"You saved me," coughs Larson with a quiet laugh.

"That's impossible," Skyler mumbles. "You were dead."

"What I saw … the Creator, she's with him. Sis…" Still kneeling, Larson bursts into tears. Skyler grabs a clean towel and hands it to him so he can clean himself up.

"Here."

"Where are you Goldberg?" Larson hiccups. "Did you see her

too? She was so beautiful, so … perfect, as if nothing had ever happened to her."

Skyler presses the towel against Larson's face. Larson's body twitches, and he jerks Skyler's wrist at lightning speed, sending a jolt through his arm.

This time, Skyler does not see his mother's face, but a girl he has never seen. She has the distinct features of the Whites, framed by long platinum hair, like Larson. The trees at the Gardens of Humanity are floating around her as she beckons him to follow. Larson stands a little farther away, holding Kahlo's hand. There are three of them. Siblings.

The lab comes back with a bang and Skyler feels like he scalded his hand in boiling water. He grabs the vial with the burn-treating medicine Larson had prepared and applies it clumsily while trying to figure out what he just saw.

How can he have a vision of someone he has never met?

How could the Whites have three children?

What happened to Kahlo and Larson's sister?

"Goldberg, why is it so dark in here? We did it. We need to celebrate. We need to…"

"I'm right here."

"Where?" asks Larson angrily as he drags himself across the floor.

Skyler watches him get up, but his balance is precarious, and he needs help. When their eyes meet, Skyler understands.

He might have come back to life, but he bears the mark of death in his irises.

Larson White is blind.

14

"It's finally the big day!"

In the crowded hallway that leads to the converted ballroom, Emily is beside herself. When he saw her earlier in the hall, he hugged her for a whole minute, relieved she didn't end up in prison.

Skyler wishes he could forget the last twenty-four hours. His parents were surprised to see him sleeping most of the day, as he usually wakes up early. He doesn't feel like celebrating, but he tries anyway. It's their graduation ceremony, after all.

The memories they share are worth celebrating. The other Archeans are now their equals, and Skyler is one step closer to his dream of following in Tamara Goldberg's footsteps. That is, if last night's mishaps don't get in the way during the mentorship selection process. He swallows hard, but Emily comes to his rescue.

"You'll never guess what happened to me," she says dramatically with an unreadable expression.

"What?" asks Skyler, concerned.

"I won't have to face the humiliation they had planned for me after graduation."

"Humiliation?"

"You know, the usual exclusively reserved-for-a-select-few mentorship kind of thing. Being a Bates, I'm pretty much prohibited from enjoying the few good things on this ship, which include a decent life supporting and keeping alive the ship that houses my tormentors. At least I won't be drudging away in a mind-numbing job."

"Because you got your art project back?" says Skyler, who remembers the bag Kahlo gave her. "Wasn't it too damaged?"

"Not at all, actually. I spent the day on it, but I still need the finishing touch."

"Great, then." His friend frowns at his lack of enthusiasm. "Seriously, I mean it."

"You don't understand. I don't dream of having a mentorship. I *have* a mentorship. A real one!"

"But how? The auction hasn't even started yet."

"Turns out my skills as an undercover agent at Adeline's soiree and my role as a secret agent for Larson's forbidden mission that led us to the Leviathan impressed Warden Yasmina Mirza. She will take me under her wing to work at the prison!"

"Is that why she wanted to talk to you in private?"

"It wasn't that simple, but I saw right through her. She made a conditional offer before the bidding for our mentorship starts. Since no one will be competing for this role, it's almost certain. Nothing will stand in Agent Emily Bates's way."

"I'm so proud of you. This will be your chance to become a tyrant instilling terror among the prisoners."

They laugh at the idea. The ship's prison will tremble at her fiery temper. Art being her one true calling, working in the prison may not be what she expected, but her background will never allow her that freedom.

Cheery, Emily scans him from head to toe.

"You know how great the Goldberg colors look on you? It's crazy how much of a difference a second-hand uniform can make, instead of the crap the Academy forces us to wear. I always feel like a shriveled-up oyster that's been out of the water for too long."

"Shells can't shrivel. The skin is a flexible membrane that adapts in the water. By shriveling up, the skin provides a more durable permeability to grip objects underwater."

"You know exactly what I mean. It's gray and ugly. The uniform is just a shell concealing our inner beauty through layers of grim fabric stifling our creativity! If art students made decisions about fashion on the Ark, their scores would dramatically improve. I'm sure Adeline White would understand my point. If she … oh my God! That's her."

The Duchess of the Ark is gleaming, adorned with a gold necklace and silver bracelets. Her pearl-studded cream gown gives her the look of a light dancer about to take off. Her outfit is just like her family: remarkable and precious. Among the teachers and parents standing at the entrance of the ballroom, Adeline White is chatting casually with Tom Harris, perfumer and Edelsa's father. He subtly brushes his arm against her several times with an easy smile.

Feeling their stares, Adeline excuses herself to her circle of admirers and floats in their direction. Skyler glances around worriedly, but she walks straight to him while briefly acknowledging Emily's presence who shrinks at her approach.

"We still have some time before the ceremony begins," Adeline says to Skyler in a low voice as she fidgets with the inlaid beads of her small velvet purse. "I think we should talk."

She clicks her heels away from the guests before he can give her an answer. Speechless, Emily waves him off.

"This is the opportunity of a lifetime. Promise me you'll tell her about me."

"What exactly do you want me to say to her?" he asks as Adeline pushes aside suitors vying to seal a new deal or simply be in her company. "I doubt it'll be a friendly meeting. She'll blame me for what happened to Larson. It could be a declaration of war between our families, for all I know." Emily looks horrified at the thought, then lets out a frustrated sigh.

"Do your best to stay alive during this meeting, then. Remember what day today is. Starting tomorrow, our new life on the Ark begins. Believe me when I say none of this will matter anymore. But for a few exceptions, people on this ship forget quickly."

"Thanks, Emily. I think Larson White's overdose and the irreversible damage to his eyesight is one of those exceptions."

"That's not what I meant. Skyler!"

Skyler sighs in annoyance, his heart heavy from the recent events. Had he been a full-fledged doctor, he wouldn't have let Larson inject himself with an unknown, life-threatening substance. He wouldn't have witnessed his madness without trying to reason with him simply because he is a White. He wouldn't have taken an even greater risk by injecting him with the unknown contents of a syringe—and not just any contents, a product from Mara, a drug dealer—which may have caused his brain damage and blindness. He used his intuition instead of his reason, ignoring everything the Academy has always taught him: to never get carried away by emotions.

Emily squeezes his shoulder in support, then Skyler weaves through the crowd that grows denser by the minute to reach the victim's mother, because that's who she is in his eyes. When misfortune strikes, it takes away the glowing titles and privileges to reveal an obvious fact clouded by greed; the Creator does not distinguish humans from one another, just as the Flood showed them a century ago.

Fortunately, his parents won't be coming to the ceremony. If they knew everything that happened, Skyler would consider himself lucky to keep the Goldberg's name, and the Creator's wrath would be nothing compared to the pain he would feel. He could live with atoning for a heavenly sin, but not knowing he caused harm to his family. They have suffered too much because of him already.

"I know this celebration is important, but it can wait a little longer," says Adeline White, with a serious face. "I hope you understand."

He nods silently lest make it worse. She motions for him to follow her down the dark side of the passageway that leads into another, quieter area.

"My two sons should have come today," she says, with the angry hissing noise coming from the clogged ventilation hatches in the background. "When I see those families laughing their heads off, unaware of the danger lurking, and thinking the Creator is watching over them and their children, it makes me sick." A hidden reader beeps when she waves her wristband. A mysterious door slides open onto the showroom she used for her exclusive party.

The once crowded place is now empty, but for the artifacts holding the secrets of an ancient civilization. Hard to believe that Skyler came here, arm in arm with Edelsa Harris, only twenty-four hours ago. He would have turned back if someone had told him what he was getting himself into by agreeing to help Emily.

"This was the only place I thought safe on the Ark. At least until one of my guests collapsed, slowly bleeding to her death. What a dreadful sight!"

The floor is glistening with disinfectant spread over the bloodstained metal. Despite Skyler's attempt at staunching the blood flow, the stain is larger than it should be. Anika's stigmata are still a mystery that eludes him.

"Your friend surprised me last night. Her colorful exit was a sight to behold."

"I didn't think you were interested in my friends."

"Goldberg, please. Keeping secrets on the Ark is an art. But enough talking about other people."

They pass by the same artifacts of the Flaminis, the strange people with prophetic visions who developed their own technology to predict the movement of the stars. The culmination of their knowledge is encapsulated in this gigantic map resting on its pedestal which dominates the room. No matter where they are, the centerpiece is clearly visible, the beauty of the mysterious engravings and symbols, unchanged.

"Kahlo is my only son who shares my obsession with these antiques. My other son, Larson, isn't the least bit interested in them. He just thinks they're a waste of our time. Isn't that what we have most on this ship? Time to occupy ourselves, to forget the sword of Damocles over our heads. An impossible paradox. I guess you're not interested in these collectibles either."

"Actually, I am. The Sigma Foundation reminds us of our past. Without them, we couldn't build our future," he says, unclear what she is getting at.

Didn't she bring him here to clarify his involvement in Larson's experiment? Why are they talking about these relics?

"You should've studied history. The Foundation would have been blessed with your vision."

In a perpendicular corridor he missed during his short visit, Adeline leads him past a dark, sphere-shaped rock protected by a glass case. It looks commonplace at first glance, but something catches his attention. He bends down to better appreciate the granular surface, polished by the seabed where thin filaments beat like steel blue blood vessels pumping blood.

"This abomination, whatever it is, will be removed from the ship tomorrow. I can't risk someone else experimenting on it. Enough people have suffered."

"The stigmata?"

"Possibly. This is the compound they found all over the lab and in Larson's blood work. The Deltas will keep a sample of this devilish rock to analyze its chemical compounds and develop the technology needed to counter its toxic effects. I will personally see to it. They may need your help in outlining the typical side effects. Can I count on you?"

"Of course," stammers Skyler, taken aback.

"Dr. Nazar told me that without your help, my son would be in the Creator's kingdom." He recognizes the emotion in Adeline's trembling voice and can only commiserate. Losing a loved one, one's own blood, is an unimaginable nightmare.

"The Creator knows what you did for my son, and I am forever grateful to him for placing you in our path."

"I couldn't stop Larson from doing his experiment. If I had stopped him, he wouldn't have—"

"Not only did you save him, but you took me to medical bay. The nurses told me everything. I wish my own son could've done it himself, but … differences can sometimes cloud reason."

She pulls a light cloth handkerchief from her small purse and awkwardly dabs at her reddened eyes.

"With Larson's current condition, the lab won't be of any use," she resumes, folding her handkerchief meticulously. "I want to give it to you as a token of my gratitude. The Whites and Goldbergs are now very close. We owe your family a great debt, and if I have the power to help their son become the next Tamara Goldberg, I will. May the Creator be my witness."

"I appreciate your gesture, but without a mentorship I won't be allowed to do research, let alone be a surgeon."

"But Dr. Nazar is your mentor! You see, I didn't have to convince him. You've proven yourself worthy of the best education this ship has to offer."

"What?"

"The auction will make it official, but it's already been agreed upon. I took care of it personally to avoid any misunderstanding. It's the least I can do."

"I don't know what to say. This is … huge."

"Sometimes there is nothing to say. Words are too small to hold the beauty of this world, however cruel it may be."

Skyler is on cloud nine as Adeline White walks him back to the ballroom. She leaves him with a promise to work out some details in the next few days about the start of his mentorship and his access to the lab. When Skyler asks if there is anything he can do to help Larson, she says, "Only time will tell. Enjoy the Creator's kindness before his mind changes."

As usual, when Adeline White enters a public place, a swarm of guests rushes over to greet her. Skyler barely has enough time to slip away. His best friend is chatting animatedly with Kahlo who bursts into laughter.

"Is everything all right over here?" smirks Skyler, glancing at Emily.

"I can't believe you were able to take that snapshot," says Kahlo, catching his breath.

"An art project deciding your fate can make you a genius overnight. Trust me," she replies, while patting the binding of a book sticking out of her bag.

"What is it?"

"See for yourself."

Skyler nabs the book, which is a photo album of their time at the Academy. She added her personal touch, of course: sketches of each student they shared laughter and tears with during all those years. Emily's unique style shows through the bright colors adorning each sketch. She could have become an artist capable of bringing back to life their slowly decaying ship with its lifeless metal walls. Perhaps her light will be able to illuminate even the corners of the Ark's prison.

"I didn't know you were a photographer in your spare time," Skyler says.

"Emily has plenty of hidden talents," says Kahlo, blushing as he pretends his cream jacket is too hot for the mediocre ventilation.

"But there's a blank page," notes Skyler, who has stumbled across an empty space.

"The final touch," answers Emily, who flies a miniature drone. "Our undercover mission had its share of emotions, but also benefits, including this little gem, courtesy of the Paragon."

"You're playing with fire," warns Skyler. "Especially for an Ark prison officer."

"I've only borrowed it for a while. Promise!"

The drone's mechanical eye locks on them while Emily is having a hell of a good time taking pictures of them striking in different, sometimes quirky, poses.

For the first time in many years, Skyler can feel alive, if only for an evening, without the Creator to remind him of the mistakes he could never fix.

15

Nothing will ever be the same.

Skyler walks through the Gardens of Humanity. The ephemeral snow melted several days ago, and the ventilation system has been repaired. Some plants, mostly grass, have turned yellow, while others have taken on a dull earth color, robbed of their fragile life by the sustained cold.

Dried clumps crackle under his footsteps as he hurries, eager to know if the flowers he discovered just before the first snowfall are still alive. It is almost impossible; many flowers are known not to resist the slightest variation in temperature, but hope guides him through the strange desolation that has settled. A blanket of snow could easily suffocate them in their crystalline beauty, but in spite of this sad knowledge, he weaves in and out of the rigid branches that shut off the small undergrowth.

The canopy is so high and tight in this corner of the park that it forms a shield against the elements: a bubble sheltered from the rest of the surrounding flora. The ground is earthy, the lack of artificial sunlight and regular sprinkling unfit for grass to thrive. But if one place could be spared from the failing ventilation, it is here.

As usual, the comforting trees' embrace brings a flood of memories of the past few days. Adeline White kept her promise to give Skyler access to her lab. Grateful for his help, Larson handed over notebooks filled with months of research that he had carefully stashed away from his mother's prying eyes.

Skyler absorbed as much information as possible to detect a flaw in Larson's bizarre experiments intended to harness this divine power he mentioned. Not having experimented himself, Skyler has no idea what it is all about, but one thing for sure is that he cannot shake off what he saw. Did some fumes in the lab give him hallucinations? Fear creeps in as he considers the possibility that a simple touch can hold such power.

Larson did extensive research in the Archives that fall under the Sigma Foundation and thus the Whites. Skyler managed to find the substance used in the dosage: a derivative of a rock found on the ocean floor. The Flaminis's ruins are full of it. Using the relic hunters' plans to re-enact this pivotal period in the Ark's foundation, Larson White took part in a hunt to get his hands on this very special rock, posing as a recruit sent by Adeline White herself. No one asked any questions. Who would want to risk their life retrieving junk from the heart of an unforgiving ocean?

The hunt was successful, and Larson kept a piece of this rock in his lab for research. While studying the molecular structure of this compound, he discovered that its liquid state was unbelievably malleable. The Flaminis's records in the Archives inspired him to create his own concoction, which, according to Larson, makes better use of its divine energy potential.

But keeping a rock in its liquid state requires a tremendous amount of energy to heat it up. He "borrowed" the energy from the Gardens of Humanity, which overheated and crashed. The temperature dropped and it snowed in the gardens, the air conditioning system unable to maintain the artificial seasons.

The most controversial conclusion of Larson's research is that the Flaminis were not charlatans. Their visions were real, the result of the Creator's memories seeping into the world. With the help of this rock, they were able to commune with this form of energy. Or so they say.

The Flaminis saw the Flood before it happened. They had a vision.

The Founders learned this too and allied themselves with the Flaminis who guided them in the construction of the Ark to save humanity from certain death.

Larson wanted to take over that ancient power. Nothing more, nothing less.

"Mrs. Farrell?"

Two baskets in her arms, the priestess of the sanctuary is bent over with one knee on the ground, scanning the undergrowth. This is the first time Skyler catches her here. Only a handful of people explore the nooks and crannies of the park.

She lifts her head, grunting something inaudible, then puts back the drooping cloth on either side of her hat, revealing her wrinkled face.

"If you weren't a Goldberg, I'd chastise you for taking me by surprise," she says, laughing in a hoarse voice. "You almost gave me a crick!"

"I'm sorry. I didn't mean to—"

"I'm kidding, boy," she replies, rising nimbly to her feet. "The Farrells would be turning in their graves of the sanctuary if aging won its eternal battle against my will. What good is a priestess overcome by the Creator's trials? Might as well bury her in the ground."

Skyler's face freezes into a half-smile, his eyebrows furrowed.

"Right. The land is getting scarce. But you know what I mean," she adds.

Her dress raises a cloud of dust and uncovers a bed of wilted flowers, frozen in a final attempt to soak in the waning artificial light, their stems twisted around themselves.

She lets out a long, weary sigh.

"I came to stock up on flowers for the sanctuary, but it looks like a tidal wave drowned them all. I'm telling you, if they took the trouble to care for those flowers, these things wouldn't happen. What fun it'll be to make those narrow-minded Believers see the truth in that! Without the Creator's miracle, they'll say that their dead can't join his Kingdom. If only they had faith, they would understand how terribly wrong they all are."

She grabs a few twigs from her basket and throws them in the air as if it were some kind of magic trick to fool the naive. A way to buy their silence and loyalty through smoke and mirrors.

"Simply ask me next time," says Skyler with a knowing smile. "I can do the picking for you. I owe you at least that much for all you've done for me."

"Don't worry about that. I must make myself useful on this ship. Between you and me, my time is better spent with anyone but those fools. May you find peace, my boy."

Mrs. Farrell flies over to a tree trunk behind Skyler and picks a red flower with her fingertips, holding it tight like a mother clutching her child with great fear in the face of danger.

"It's a way to drag me out of my den, as my granddaughter would say," she breathes, almost wistfully. "My grandchildren are more than pleased whenever I go out to get some fresh air. I can understand that. I, for one, wanted my independence early, boy. *Very* early. Like a bud peeking out in the middle of winter."

"You speak as if you have already experienced it. Winter."

"Our ancestors, yes, and through their memories, so can we remember. The Creator's gift is powerful. You just need to know how to use it. To no one's surprise, most of this ship has forgotten how to do it. Come on, boy, I have to get back to reassure them. God knows how easily they can come up with another godly message or some holy martyr of who-knows-what."

"May the Creator protect us."

"You bet!"

The priestess' dress sends a cloud of golden earth hanging in the tangy air. A surprise awaits Skyler when he walks back into the undergrowth.

Blue hydrangeas. The special thing about these flowers is that they grow directly on a shrub, in clusters that look like spheres.

He gets closer to the flower bush where each petal is connected in a complex network. His memories carry him to a habitable land, where all living things are intertwined.

Perhaps this connection between him and Larson truly happened. So did the Flaminis and the Founders. The Creator might do the same in his own way, whether through cryptic messages, symbols, or the Ark's priestess.

Larson White might have been stupid and blinded by his desires to change the Ark. The Believers might be desperate for a way to see the Creator's manifestation, or some proof that he has not abandoned them.

The Creator's gift is powerful. You just need to know how to use it.

Aren't they all looking for the same thing? That connection through those memories they cherish so much? Has there ever been a time in the history of their civilization when they felt so alone, abandoned by their own Creator?

The ebb and flow of time eventually take away their memories of who they are and their place in this world that has shunned them. But to have a fighting chance at seeking redemption for their past mistakes, the Archeans cannot forget, for forgetting is the beginning of folly.

Larson was separated from his sister, and when he saw her in his vision, he just knew. He remembered his place, his role, the path to sanity. Skyler knows deep down that this is true. This was possible from remembering and feeling that connection with her. A miracle. The Creator's gift.

Eyes shut; Skyler lets his mind drift in the sweet, honeyed smell of hydrangeas.

What if there was a way to preserve these memories—the memories of their humanity—for eternity?

END OF THE PREQUEL

THE ADVENTURE CONTINUES IN...

BOOK 1

AFTERWORD

Thank you so much for boarding the Ark with me!

Did you know your reviews make it possible to sell books?

If you liked this novel, I would appreciate it if you could leave a review on your preferred platform.

Also, I love to talk to my readers, so don't hesitate to send me a message directly at davidmsnow@davidmsnow.com.

Don't forget to subscribe to my Readers' Club on my website to receive the latest updates and exclusive content.

www.davidmsnow.com

Thank you and see you on the Ark!

ACKNOWLEDGMENTS

This prequel was not planned originally, but it was necessary. I was able to spend an unforgettable time with Skyler and Emily before the tragic events of the series happened. It allowed me to catch my breath, especially after having written the first two books. I hope you had as much fun reading as I did writing it.

I would first like to thank Pascal Raud, my awesome developmental editor who is exceptional! Not only is he a mentor, but also a friend who knows how to tap on the potential of a manuscript and this prequel is no exception. It's so handy to have someone who can read my mind and pick the right word to express what I am trying to say. His comments have greatly improved the flow of this book along with my writing skills. It's now my turn to challenge him to write his first novel. Get ready!

My best friend Kim Archambault for all our conversations that rekindle my passion for writing even when self-doubt sets in. She nourishes a deep passion for writing, and she's the best when it comes to brainstorming crazy ideas.

My beta readers Mélissa Lemaire, a fan of the series, and Célia Chalfoun, a friend whose editing skills are unparalleled.

The copyeditor of this book, Heidi Ripplinger, who polished this piece with her insightful comments and clarity.

Special thanks to my parents for their unshakable support. They have always believed in my projects even when I had given up.

My partner who puts up with my blank stares and my hours of silence while I'm busy writing my next novel.

I want to say thank you to my readers for keeping my passion for writing alive and pushing me to become a better author. Without you, writing wouldn't mean the same. I can't wait to share more stories with you in the *very* near future.

See you soon!

David M. Snow

EXCERPT: AMARANTH BOOK 1

CHAPTER 1 SKYLER

Every breath is agony and the wait, unbearable. For a moment, the man seems to be free of his illness, but at the last second, he gasps in a large gulp of air, as if he were about to drown.

Skyler monitors his patient's irregular vital signs closely.

The Fairies have been relentless with their victim this time. They are unpredictable, and especially cunning. They will now enrapture the man by luring him into their invisible realm. It's a one-way ticket. First, the Fairies induce dreams of a world where anything is possible, where the Flood never happened. The dreams are a little longer each time, and then the harrowing of hell begins.

There is no shame in being tempted. Even Skyler would like a second chance.

But fairies do not exist, of course.

The pungent stink of solvent wafting off the patient is Skyler's cue to prepare the procedure. Everything must be ready before the man slips to the other side. It's a swift process, only a few minutes, and every second is crucial.

Skyler leaves the man momentarily to gather what he needs for the next step. He makes his way through cases of pharmaceuticals—mostly painkillers—to the back of the circular room, where sits a recessed cabinet. He holds his breath and drags open a large, heavy cabinet drawer, its worn metal screeching, where a dozen remaining spheres each lie on its cushion, asleep, waiting for a host. The missing spheres are already buzzing with life in the Archives. Skyler makes a mental note to hit up the warehouse of the medical bay soon and replenish his supply.

He smiles at the gentle coolness of transparent glass in his palm. This is a victory that will change the course of history.

He closes the drawer, taking care not to damage the remaining spheres. They are invaluable, the result of many years of research and heated debates with his mentor, Dr. Nazar.

Skyler walks back to the dying man as Mira scribbles a few notes. His colleague's skin is strikingly pale, her freckles almost invisible in the stinging overhead light that dissolves all color in its path. Delta Division should have taken care of the ward's poor lighting by now, but just as with every other request aboard the Ark, Skyler would have to be patient.

He fits the sphere into the depression that feeds into the encephalogram at the head of the bed: its integrated touch screen lights up with interlocking curves. Skyler prepares the calibration by checking the signature of the host's brain activity: an array of unique frequencies, much like a fingerprint, that the system recognizes.

"I'm not sure I understand," Mira says to Skyler as she moves closer to the monitor, pen in hand.

"Make sure you adjust the sphere to the brain's maximum and minimum frequencies," he explains, pointing to numbers on the screen. "If you want any chance of encoding all their memories, be as accurate as possible. Averaging the data out won't do. You must scan all data from the last twenty-four hours."

"The system's measurements aren't good?"

"It tends to leave out sudden variations. But even minor variation is important to storing all the memories. If the range of data is too wide, it introduces too much interference, making it impossible to tell one memory from another."

"Good to know."

A muffled moan draws their attention. The man is in critical condition.

"Get ready."

As always, the wait is unnerving, but also deeply sad. Even though they were trained to remain emotionally distant from their patients, Skyler can't help but feel a twinge of sadness for Francisco. The poor man has no one to spend his last moments with. No family to care for him.

When the Fairies do their work, though, the victim doesn't feel regret. Quite the opposite; it's all blank looks and blissful smiles; a hollow happiness towards death.

A long, hoarse sigh brings a sickening acrid smell. Francisco is no more.

"Now!" Skyler says firmly. He supervises Mira as she initiates the transfer.

Four minutes. It only takes four minutes to extract the entirety of someone's lived experiences. It doesn't seem long enough, but it can be done.

Sparks escape from the center of the awakening sphere. They become long, hair-like strands that diffuse into the water, twisting and entangling as they swirl counter-clockwise.

If only the many who had preceded Francisco in death could have had the same chance. The lived experiences of every Archean are invaluable to those who will repopulate the Earth. Their ancestors fought to survive, but what has become of their joys, sorrows, fears—their stories? What made them human?

Forgotten. Every last one of them.

The swirling finally slows, and the emitted glow deepens, which means the transfer is complete. The sphere fills with a scarlet light, hallmark to the disease's victory. It is the individual's electrical frequencies that determine the light's hue: a biological signature unique to each individual, one that cannot deceive. However, the Fairy Syndrome alters this signature although no one knows why yet, but Skyler intends to find out. On his own, of course, since Delta Division will never get involved—they have other priorities.

"Do you have any more questions?" he asks, dropping the still-warm sphere into a cushioned carrying case he's pulled from the cabinet.

"I think I'm okay," she replies, while she finishes jotting down some notes. "I just need to try by myself next time."

"You'll be all right," he says with an encouraging smile. "You've always been one of the most competent people here."

"Is this even worth it?" snaps a voice he wishes he hadn't heard. Chris. The son of the Paragon general of the Theta Division, Duke Kay. Top of their class, he was spoiled for choice; he could have joined the ranks of an army ready to answer to him at the drop of a hat, but instead, he makes their lives a living hell in med bay. No doubt his father couldn't handle him either.

"I mean, going to all this trouble for a bunch of average people who lead mind-numbing lives?" adds Chris, who crosses his arms, his perfect face warped by its usual sneer as he glares at him. Despite being in his early twenties, his cheeks are still as smooth as a child's, giving him a deceptively innocent look.

"And your life is more worthy?"

"My knowledge of modern medicine will be useful for future generations. As for him," says Chris, pointing at the dead patient with a disgusted look, "the Syndrome has already affected his brain beyond repair. Do you really want future generations to remember his bouts of madness? What's the point?"

"What if it's the key to saving us? All of us?" asks Skyler, his fingers clenching the box of Francisco's memories. Chris snorts with an amused half-smile.

"Don't take your dreams for granted. Just because Dr. Siria supports your ideas doesn't mean they'll make any difference."

"At least I'm trying to make sense of our work. For all of us." Chris gets close enough that his breath grazes Skyler's chin.

Skyler doesn't flinch. Chris has been the same ever since he can remember and Skyler avoids him as much as possible, ignores him even, but working together complicates things. Why does Chris go to such lengths? If he put as much work into caring for his patients as he does for himself, no one would have to work overtime.

A glint flashes through Chris's eyes. Is he enjoying himself?

"You're wasting your time," Duke's son scoffs. "This Syndrome is a fate that we must accept. It is a fair response to our sins."

Mira blinks and stares at each of them. Chris thinks he has the answer to everything—a trait he borrows from his father—but if anyone should spend more time in the sanctuary pondering his sins, it should be him. Has he ever actually been there? That would be a surprise. His family is not known for its piety. Even his own mother didn't have a proper funeral.

"How would you know?"

"It's not rocket science, Sky. You disappoint me. You really do. I thought you'd be more perceptive, but by the looks of it, sympathizing with these weaklings has affected you."

"I don't have to answer to you, so get out of my way. I got work to do." Chris thinks, blocking Skyler's path, for a long while—so long, in fact, that Skyler considers pushing him out of his way. But then Chris steps over ever so slightly.

A missed opportunity. There will be more.

"Somehow, I understand Dr. Nazar," Chris says thoughtfully as Sky heads down the hall. "I would have given up too, just to avoid listening to your grumbling."

"Yeah, whatever," says Skyler, his back turned, ready to leave. Mira asks Chris to stop, but Skyler doesn't dwell. It's always the same with Chris. He's been opposed to this project from the beginning arguing that the memory spheres should be for those who truly deserve them. Well, that's not for him to judge.

Everyone deserves a chance.

The harsh lighting of med bay gives way to the dim light of the corridor, which mimics the amber glow of dusk—or at least dusk as it's described at the Academy. Skyler rubs his burning eyes, another telltale sign that the ship is contaminated by poorly-filtered underwater oxygen. His father often complains about the problems with ventilation and high humidity that he and his colleagues in the Delta division, the Ark's largest division, have to deal with.

Skyler narrowly avoids a puddle as he enters the nearest elevator. The condensation beads lining the doors glow dimly in the evening light. He takes a seat among a few civilian Archeans, decked in Delta uniforms, chatting quietly. Deltas are found almost everywhere, given the considerable burden of maintaining the ship and its equipment. Skyler gently releases his grip from the case he has been carrying, his hands sore and fingers stiff from clutching it so tightly. He brushes over the numbered buttons on the elevator with his fingertips. Those for the dining room and cabins are faded, but number seven is clearly visible, shiny even. He presses it.

Chris's jab has dampened his spirits. If only Chris could stop making his life insufferable… He lost Skyler's trust in the past and his snarky remarks only make it worse.

The metallic creaking of the elevator is not exactly reassuring, but life on a century-old Ark isn't without its flaws.

He becomes aware of a baby near him crying, a bitter reminder of how uncertain their future is. Not only might this shabby elevator never make it to the top, but they might never make it out of the ship alive.

Upon reaching the seventh floor, Skyler follows the hallway towards two large glass doors and crosses two Paragon agents on silent patrol, their electric batons in plain sight, who pay little attention to him. He is asked to identify himself by a computer-generated voice and scans the wristband he's worn since birth. He's immediately granted access and the doors slide open, emitting a cool breeze that gives him shivers.

Welcome to the Archives of Humanity. May you be granted salvation.

If only it were that easy. Machines have an uncanny ability to take words intended to be comforting and render them meaningless.

The lobby of the highly protected Archives flaunts a swarm of surveillance cameras and concealed doors. There is a sacred feel to this place that houses everything the Archeans know about their ancestors' world. It bathes in a diffused light with a simple corridor leading to a spacious circular room, where an equally spacious and circular reception desk marks center stage. The other employees do not notice him, with the exception of the young girl who usually prepares his Nave. They exchange a smile, but nothing more.

The Nave is blinking at him, but he's already used up all the time allotted to him this month. Taking in the fragments of the lost world in these private cabins can be an intoxicating experience. Limiting their time is a silly rule, since hardly anyone comes here, but the Naves are few and should be available to all authorized personnel.

Skyler walks closer to the dark, slightly raised granite counter lit by a bluish backlight against a dark background which is not what you would expect for a place like the Archives. It contains no physical books, since most of them were washed away. Those that were digitized before the Flood remain in servers stored here while the rest are lost forever.

Dr. Siria is not here, but, knowing her, she can't be too far.

He crosses the large room and slips through the dark hall that leads to a seemingly invisible corridor; due to some optical illusion, black on black, it perfectly deceives prying eyes. A faint light at the end is all that guides him as he passes through.

A smell of newly-heated plastic wafts through the air of the room specially-equipped for his memory spheres project. The spheres are stored and decoded here. For now, there's nothing too impressive, just a terminal and a repository that collects the spheres, which can reveal the memories of past existences. At least that's what Nathan claims, the Delta engineer breaking protocol to help them.

"So soon?" Dr. Siria greets him, her gaze shifting from the terminal screen to the box. "Had I known there would be so many, I would have reconsidered your request."

"Should I just stop everything now?" he replies defensively, Chris's jab still hurting.

"Don't take it the wrong way," she laughs as he opens the box over the receptacle.

The threads within the sphere spin lazily, casting a glowing waltz of reddish light that dances on the walls of the dark room. Dr. Siria stares wantingly at the sphere, mesmerized, and moves in to take a closer look.

"I would have better prepared, that's all. It is a great privilege to add these to the collection." The glow casts curious shadows on the face of Valentina Siria, the only doctor daring enough to support his project from the beginning. Although Sky likes his mentor, Dr. Nazar has been skeptical, and Dr. Siria had to convince him by assuming all the risk.

"At least these people won't be forgotten," he says, reluctantly leaving the fragile globe in the care of his patron, who places it into the receptacle which swallows the sphere whole.

The room loses the warm glow that gave it life and only the cold remains.

"We will soon have to make sure our efforts are not in vain," adds Skyler, breaking the contemplative silence that had settled. "Though how we might do so eludes me."

"We must not lose hope," she answers, a faint smile on her lips. "If our ancestors had given in to despair, we wouldn't be together here today discussing this."

How much longer will they have to hang on to hope? Repopulating is unlikely at this time, and the memory spheres are still in their infancy. Not to mention the resilience of the Syndrome taking hold.

How can you defeat an enemy that does not exist?

CHAPTER 2 EMILY

Fiona Reyes. The fresh case that adds to the dozens of prisoners being held for crimes that range from stealing food from the dining hall to corruption. But her situation is special.

Fiona Reyes is a Maverick.

She didn't come alone. There was this other guy with her, Milo. No last name: You don't need one when you're a Maverick. It's a waste of time. Even if he had one, no one would remember it. But this Reyes has something just as interesting as her last name: her arrogance. The report said she struggled with and spat on the officers handling her case, that she was missing that bewildered look so characteristic of other Mavericks who were caught in the last few years.

Emily walks down the main corridor to the cell block, two steaming coffees in her hands. She takes a right into a secluded passage. The only door here is ajar and Emily steps inside. The office is empty, but it doesn't matter. Yasmina seemed troubled this morning in her email about Reyes. Catching Mavericks always does that to her. Emily puts one cup down on the workstation. Caffeine should help Yasmina get through this one; maybe even calm her down.

Emily walks back out of the office and heads towards the cells, which are sealed off by a heavy double door that could literally withstand anything. Her own wristband doesn't even allow her in.

"It must have been a long night," Emily says. She hands the second cup of black coffee to the guard, who takes a sip. His pallid face brightens up a little. He suddenly looks younger.

"Good luck with this one," Ludo tells her. "It wasn't easy to shut her up." His hair and eyebrows are almost white, though he is too young to go gray. Is it because of some trauma he had in his childhood? Despite the white hair, his skin has a dark tint that sucks all his colors into an impenetrable clump. He is hard to read, but not impossible. Right now he's pissed, most likely because of this Reyes.

"You didn't give her too much tranquilizer?" she asks, raising her eyebrows.

"Only what she needs." He has a sneer hanging on his lips, his eyes sparkling.

"Look," she adds, seeing that he doesn't approve. "It's difficult to interrogate someone who's high." He grunts his consent, then lets her into what they call the Hall of the Forgotten.

Ludo clams up when he feels threatened. The last time, he didn't speak to her again for an entire week. But they have to work together, so his cooperation is vital. Not so long ago, he drugged a prisoner to the point of forgetting his own name. Ludo's methods are questionable because they encroach on Emily's interrogations. Writing up a satisfactory prisoner psychological profile is no small feat. And submitting a botched report … it's better not to think about it.

Emily's steps echo over the buzzing sound of the overhead ducts. A firm step. It is paramount to be in complete control of yourself, just in case. She must work without the protection of a guard to minimize interference with the analysis. She couldn't focus properly otherwise. A stolid attitude works wonders with inmates who think they can coax her out; they come up against a wall even stronger than the cell that confines them.

A screen buzzes up as Emily halts in front of cell number twenty-four: She lays a hand on it. The prisoner had her long, black hair turned to the surveillance camera. Will she pounce like a rabid animal?

A beep signals the scanner has read her wristband and Emily enters the cell.

The sound of the door as it closes seems to suck the air out of the cell along with it. A muffled thud replaces the buzzing sound from earlier. The young prisoner bursts into a throaty laugh. A chill runs down Emily's spine.

"They're already sending one of their elite agents," says Fiona Reyes, facing the opposite wall. "They sure aren't wasting any time." Reyes stares at the unadorned wall, the same drab walls that line the entire interior of the ship, metal plates interlocked in a lifeless maze. These cells look every bit like the Bates cabin, minus the clutter. They are oppressive. Even more so when … no, don't think about it.

Emily swallows hard. Her throat stiffens dangerously, her lungs short of breath.

She hates this place.

"No, they aren't. And the sooner you talk, the sooner this will be over," she says, swallowing a gulp of air.

"I'm not saying anything if I can't see Milo." That prisoner with no last name? So they can work out an escape plan?

"You're in no position to negotiate anything." Reyes looks back at Emily, arms folded. She is stone-faced.

"You want to know where the other Mavericks are, right?" says Reyes casually.

"Obviously."

"If I tell you, can I see Milo?" She's so persistent … is he her boyfriend or something? Why give in so soon? Not so clever for a Maverick.

"Is that all you want?"

"If that's what it'll take to get some peace in here, why not? It's not like it's a secret to anyone." Reyes stares back at her. Her sunken cheeks exaggerate her prominent cheekbones.

"So where are they?"

"You gotta promise you'll bring me to him."

"Fine," says Emily matter-of-factly. "If that'll get you to talk." Too easy. What's going on in her head? If only Emily knew Reyes' color, she could make a guess about her true intentions. Come on, focus, Emily.

"Everywhere," says Reyes. Emily slowly circles the prisoner who watches her. The colors are quiet today.

Reyes eyeballs her. Can she hear what Emily is hearing?

"They're everywhere," Reyes repeats, hands on her hips. "There's your answer. Now I want to see Milo."

"You're lying," says Emily, coming to a stop. The air ripples around the inmate, her throaty laughter bouncing against the gray walls of the cell. Some variations are taking shape, coming off of her dark hair, some kind of feeling. A little more, and the color of her aura will show itself.

Emily walks around the prisoner again.

"And how can you be so sure?" Reyes asks out of sheer bravado. "You know nothing about me."

"Enough to know that you wouldn't give up that kind of information so easily." Reyes' hesitation reveals dancing pink edges around her dark hair.

"That's not the answer you want, but I don't want to waste my time with you," Reyes insists with a falsely smug look.

"How great is that? Me neither," retorts Emily as she heads for the door. "Now you know what to expect for my next visit."

"Hey, wait!" Reyes' dismay is palpable.

A horrid chill runs down Emily's spine. For a second, her

body is not her own. Her skin is blinding white, freckles ravage her forearms. Her hair lengthens, burning her shoulders, a luminous shine that could be mistaken for fire. No! She's not giving in now.

"Sorry, I'm on a pretty tight schedule," says Emily in a softer voice.

"You promised I could see Milo," Reyes yells. A concealed dread is burrowing in her eyes. That is how prisoners feel around Emily.

Her mouth is pasty and her face is numb.

"I didn't promise anything," Emily says, staring straight into her eyes. The echo of her own words sounds oddly familiar.

Emily turns away to step out of the cell. She doesn't see the blow coming and she is thrown against the opposite wall. Blinded by rage, Fiona has her in a choke hold. Emily backs up hard and wedges her attacker against the wall. Fiona tightens her hold, but Emily headbutts her enough to loosen her fingers. Emily grabs the arm pressing against her throat and hurls Fiona to the ground. In an instant, Reyes is incapacitated, face down, her arm locked behind her back.

"Don't you ever touch me again," warns Emily in a whisper.

"Go to hell!" spits Reyes.

"Nothing's stopping me from finishing you off right here and now. So, answer my question. Where are the Mavericks hiding?"

"I … told you … already," sputters Reyes under the weight of the foot on her back.

"If that's what you want…" Fiona cries out in pain as Emily jerks her back up hard. She throws her back into the cell and seals the door immediately. Her muscles remain stiff as she tries to calm herself down, Reyes' laugh still buzzing in her head.

Inexplicable tremors shake through her body. She sits against the wall to collect herself. Ludo cannot see her like this or he will report it to Yasmina. The last person to upset on this Ark.

The weight of Reyes' mangled body in her hands … *by* her hands … lingers. Her own safety had been put at risk. Nothing else could have saved her.

Emily rubs her wet cheeks with the back of her hand. Now's not the time.

She walks back down the Hall of the Forgotten and tries to clear her mind. A surprise attack is always unnerving. Given Reyes' resistance during her capture, it was almost obvious that she would try something. This is not the first time this has happened. Reyes didn't stand a chance.

Why can't her muscles relax?

She lets out a sigh. Hot, burning.

Her nails dig into her palms and she slows her pace as she nears the gate. She glances at cell number twenty-four.

The Mavericks… They must be well-organized to stay off the radar and elude the watchful eye of the Paragon. Yet it is surprising that they are still alive after all these years shut off in the lower levels. But since the Incident, combing through those parts has become more than an issue. What if…?

Ludo looks surprised to see her back so soon. He gulps down the rest of his large coffee.

"Cut down her rations for two days," says Emily without stopping.

He doesn't reply. Ludo's gaze follows her gesture to wipe the corner of her lips where blood is beading. Suddenly, she can make out Fiona Reyes' aura: pink. But not any pink: the same shade some flowers that used to grow on Earth had … but not anymore, of course, since everything flooded over. Reyes' color, difficult to perceive, is now clear. Clear enough, at least, to know exactly what kind of person she is.

She was not lying.

On her way to the elevator, Emily waves her wristband and moves through a circular machine that detects any objects she may have on her. All these procedures are such a pain.

Sometimes, she wonders who the actual prisoners are.

ABOUT THE AUTHOR

David M. Snow is a science-fiction and fantasy author for adults. When he is not busy reading with a cup of green tea, running 5km, looking up new words in the dictionary for hours on end, or learning Mandarin, Tagalog, Japanese or Korean, he sits down with his MacBook Pro and types his next novel in a frenzy.

With a Master's in Applied Linguistics and more than five years of teaching experience, he is also a linguist, polyglot, entrepreneur and teacher. After spending several years in China, he is in search of new places to explore.